Jesus had Judas...
Caesar had Brutus...
Dangerous men you'll agree...
Second-rate enemies...
I don't fear such as these...
The feller what scares me is me...

Monroe D. Underwood

THE RADISH RIVER CAPER

- A CHANCE PURDUE MYSTERY -

ROSS H. SPENCER

DIVERSIONBOOKS

Also by Ross H. Spencer

Kirby's Last Circus
Death Wore Gloves

The Chance Purdue Series
The Dada Caper
The Reggis Arms Caper
The Stranger City Caper
The Abu Wahab Caper

The Lacey Lockington Series
The Fifth Script
The Devereaux File
The Fedorovich File

Diversion Books
A Division of Diversion Publishing Corp.
443 Park Avenue South, Suite 1008
New York, New York 10016
www.DiversionBooks.com

For more information, email info@diversionbooks.com

First Diversion Books edition March 2015.
Print ISBN: 978-1-62681-965-8
eBook ISBN: 978-1-62681-654-1

This book is dedicated to Robert L. Fish.
If I could write like Robert L. Fish
I wouldn't be writing like Ross H. Spencer.

1

...as I figger it Methuselah could of had over three hunnert thousand hangovers...

Monroe D. Underwood

I sat on the steps of the Brownleaf Avenue Public Library and fired up a crooked Camel.

Out on Brownleaf the big trucks went by belching noise and plumes of black diesel smoke.

In a hurry to go and in a hurry to get back.

Like mice in little wire wheels.

Progress.

As good a name as any.

They have to call it something.

An elderly lady came out of the library.

She wore a long black dress and high-topped shoes.

Her snowy hair was a bright white beacon in the September morning sunlight.

I glanced at my watch.

Ten-thirty.

Hepzibah Dodd was right on the money.

She passed within three feet of me.

She carried a polka-dot umbrella and a copy of *An Inquiry Into the Nature and Causes of the Wealth of Nations.*

By Adam Smith.

Leave it to a guy named Smith to come up with a title like that.

Anybody else would have called the damn thing "$."

I watched Hepzibah Dodd hobble across Brownleaf Avenue.

She entered the Fall Out Inn at the corners of Brownleaf and Amsterdam.

I got up and followed.

She was parked in a booth near a wall telephone.

She was browsing through *An Inquiry Into the Nature and Causes of the Wealth of Nations.*

By Adam Smith.

I sat at the bar and kept tabs on her reflection in the backbar mirror.

A waitress brought her a martini.

I ordered a bottle of Old Washensachs and nursed it along until I saw the old gal go to work on her olive.

Then I walked to a rickety telephone booth in the rear.

I took out my notebook and dialed the number Mrs. Jonesberry had given me.

The phone rang twice.

A familiar high-pitched nasal voice said hi there whoever.

I said Mrs. Jonesberry this is Chance Purdue reporting in.

Mrs. Jonesberry said Chance who?

I said Purdue.

I said like the university.

I said Purdue with the Big Ten.

Mrs. Jonesberry said young man I think you're bragging.

I said Mrs. Jonesberry you hired me last night on the telephone.

Mrs. Jonesberry said oh of course.

She said the private detective.

She said have you picked up the trail of Hepzibah Dodd?

I said nothing to it.

I said she was in the library just like you figured.

I said now she's in a tavern at Brownleaf and Amsterdam.

Mrs. Jonesberry said what's she doing?

I said she's eating an olive and reading *An Inquiry Into the Nature and Causes of the Wealth of Nations.*

I said by Adam Smith.

I peered through the murky window of the telephone booth.

I said scratch that.

I said now she's on the phone.

I chuckled.

I said probably getting a bet down.

Mrs. Jonesberry whistled.

She said Purdue you're a clever devil.

I said so what do I do now?

Mrs. Jonesberry said wait until she gets off the phone and ask her for a match.

She said approach her just as you would approach a young and beautiful woman.

I said whoa.

I said Mrs. Jonesberry what's this all about?

I said I don't want to end up in bed with Methuselah's

great-grandmother.

Mrs. Jonesberry's high-pitched nasal voice took on a raspy edge.

She said Purdue when I phoned for your services I didn't ask questions did I?

I said no ma'am.

Mrs. Jonesberry said you're going to get paid aren't you?

I shrugged.

I said okay Mrs. Jonesberry.

Mrs. Jonesberry said that's much better.

She said Hepzibah Dodd is a very hot old number.

She said she'll probably invite you right up to her apartment.

I said but my God she got fifty years on Grandma Moses.

Mrs. Jonesberry said Grandma Moses is dead.

I said I stand on my statement.

Mrs. Jonesberry said Purdue that's twice goddammit.

I said sorry Mrs. Jonesberry.

Mrs. Jonesberry said you are to accompany Hepzibah Dodd with no discussion whatsoever.

I shrugged.

I said well that's probably for the best.

I said there's nothing we could discuss anyway.

I said the Civil War is over.

I said the North won.

Mrs. Jonesberry sighed.

She said I'll be in contact with you very soon.

She said any questions?

I said you better believe it.

I said how do I get out of Hepzibah Dodd's apartment?

Mrs. Jonesberry hung up.

I shrugged.

Well what the hell.

Seventy-five bucks was seventy-five bucks.

I came out of the telephone booth as Hepzibah Dodd left the wall phone and tottered back to her seat.

I shoved a bent Camel into my mouth and sauntered slowly in her direction.

She was watching me out of the corner of her eye.

She put a hand to her white hair.

I said hi toots you got a match?

Hepzibah Dodd smiled a faded smile.

She picked up her copy of *An Inquiry Into the Nature and Causes of the Wealth of Nations.*

By Adam Smith.

She stood and grabbed my arm.

She had a grip like a brand-new bear trap.

Her voice was quavery.

She said of course big boy.

She said in my apartment.

2

...sex is here to stay...where else could it be so important?...

Monroe D. Underwood

Hepzibah Dodd steered me out of the tavern.

We rounded the corner.

I helped her up a flight of stairs.

Her apartment was directly above the Fall Out Inn.

It was spacious and quiet and luxuriously furnished.

She put down her copy of *An Inquiry Into the Nature and Causes of the Wealth of Nations.*

By Adam Smith.

She said I'll be right with you.

She pushed me into an overstuffed chair.

She said make yourself comfortable stud.

She winked at me.

She whistled.

I managed a ghastly smile.

I watched her go into a bedroom and close the door.

Ten-to-one she'd come out in something sheer.

I tried not to think about it.

I thought about it anyway.

I shuddered.

Not me by God.

This was above and beyond the call of duty and I already had one Bronze Star.

I started to leave.

I heard the bedroom door swing open behind me.

Too late my God too late.

A soft husky-sweet voice said Purdue will you come back here and sit down goddammit?

I turned.

Brandy Alexander was wearing a brown robe.

There would be absolutely nothing under it but Brandy Alexander.

If I knew Brandy Alexander.

I knew Brandy Alexander very well.

She stood in the bedroom doorway running a comb through her thick dark wavy hair.

She said Jesus Christ Purdue how I hate disguises.

Her liquid brown eyes danced and she smiled her wonderfully warm smile.

I sat down.

Brandy said hi there.

I said hi Brandy.

Brandy said how like a winter hath my absence been from thee.

She said Shakespeare.

I shrugged.

I said roses are red violets are blue.

I said Everybody.

I said except maybe Adam Smith.

I said where the hell is Hepzibah Dodd?

Brandy's voice became quavery.

She said I'm Hepzibah Dodd.

She shifted her voice an octave upward into a nasal gear.

She said I'm also Mrs. Jonesberry.

She threw back her lovely head and laughed musically.

I said uh-huh.

I looked at the floor.

I said &@#$%¢*!

Brandy said aw Purdue it was a necessary test.

She said don't take it to heart.

I said who's taking it to heart?

I said where's my seventy-five bucks?

Brandy sat on the arm of my chair.

She leaned over.

Her face was very close to mine.

Her lilac perfume nearly blew my clutch.

Her voice was lush brown velvet.

She said Purdue you're going to get your seventy-five dollars.

She said but baby you're going to earn every dime of it.

Her robe had come open.

There was absolutely nothing under it but Brandy Alexander.

She kissed me with warm soft red lips.

She said do you know what that means?

I shrugged.

I said it means you're going to postpone reading *An Inquiry Into the Nature and Causes of the Wealth of Nations.*

I said by Adam Smith.

3

...love is the only four-letter word which nobody knows what it means...

Monroe D. Underwood

I arrived at my office at dusk.

My office was the third booth at Wallace's Tavern.

It still is.

Wallace brought me a bottle of Old Washensachs.

He said are you as bushed as you look?

I said I'm too bushed to discuss it.

I sat there nipping at my beer and thinking about Brandy Alexander.

There was just no telling when she would pop up.

Or where.

I'd met her the previous December.

Then she had slipped out of my life for six months.

She had made a pair of memorable appearances in June and that had been it until now.

And already she was gone again.

Brandy owned Confidential Investigations downtown.

She was a crackerjack operative with a wealth of CIA training.

She still handled certain CIA assignments.

She had saved Betsy's life in December.

She had saved mine in June.

She was fire and ice and she was brilliant.

She had the tawny body of a cougar.

She had the grace and reflexes to go with it.

And the claws.

She was dynamite in or out of bed and she was undoubtedly the most beautiful brunette on the face of Planet Earth.

She was the only thoroughly practical female I'd ever met.

She didn't believe that people should own people but she saw no evil in occasional short-term loans.

She was in love with me.

She admitted it frankly.

She had never asked if I loved her.

I had never told her that I did because I didn't know how Brandy looked at love.

I had never told her that I didn't because I knew how I saw it.

I would explain this.

But I'm married.

4

...suicide ain't nothing but a shortcut to where you
would of probly wound up anyway...

Monroe D. Underwood

It was pushing midnight.

Wallace came over with another bottle of Old
Washensachs.

My tenth.

Or fifteenth.

Give or take a few.

Wallace said you got anything going just now?

I shrugged.

I said I was on a case earlier today.

I said I blew it.

I said my client was very satisfied.

Wallace gave me a look and went away.

I lit a busted Camel and listened to Old Dad Underwood
and Shorty Connors discuss bowling.

Old Dad Underwood said lift is of the utmost importance in bowling.

He said you got to raise your bowling arm very high so you look like the Statue of Liberty.

He said of course you must be careful not to raise your other arm in the same fashion on account of people will think you are being held up and they will call the police.

Shorty Connors said it is unwise to raise your bowling arm very high until you have rolled several balls.

Old Dad Underwood said I never roll several balls.

He said I just roll the same ball several times.

Shorty Connors said if you raise your bowling arm very high before you have rolled several balls you are likely to wind up with a rupture.

Old Dad Underwood said for your information a rupture is no longer referred to as a rupture.

He said a rupture is now referred to as a hernia.

Shorty Connors said well no matter how you refer to a rupture you can bowl a whole mess of games for what it costs to get a hernia fixed.

A big red-faced guy came in.

He glanced at the sign above the third booth.

He walked over to me.

He said I'm looking for Chance Purdue.

I gritted my teeth.

I said there's more to it than that.

I said you are also standing on his toe.

I said try to get off as soon as possible.

I said it hurts like hell.

The big red-faced guy got off.

He grinned apologetically.

He said sorry.

I said two minds with but a single thought.

I grabbed my foot.

The big red-faced guy sat down.

I unlaced my shoe.

I said Jesus Christ you're heavy.

The big red-faced guy said I'm Suicide Lewisite.

I took off my shoe.

I caressed my toe.

I said there there baby.

Suicide Lewisite said I'm head coach of the Radish River Possumcats.

I put my shoe back on.

I said I think you missed your calling.

I said you should be smashing grapes in some winery.

I said preferably in Upper Maroovia.

Suicide Lewisite said we're a minor league football team.

He said we blew our opener to Rhubarb Ridge 52-0 and we lost the next one to Sassafras Valley 51-0.

I said well cheer up.

I said already you're showing improvement.

Suicide Lewisite said may God be with us when we play Cranberry Creek Saturday night.

I said I didn't know God was interested in football.

Suicide Lewisite said oh he just got to be.

He said how else do you explain eighty thousand perfectly normal people coming out in a blizzard and paying ten dollars a copy to get double pneumonia while watching a game none of them understands which is played by a herd of overgrown numbskulls pursuing a ball that won't even bounce straight?

I said I suppose I'm expected to ask how come they call you Suicide.

Suicide Lewisite said oh it ain't compulsory or nothing like that.

He said but almost everybody does.

I shrugged.

I said okay how come they call you Suicide?

Suicide Lewisite said because suicide is a time-honored tradition in the Lewisite family.

He said the only Lewisite that didn't commit suicide was my grandfather.

He said my grandfather got killed by a truck when he was five years old.

I said wait a minute.

Suicide Lewisite nodded and threw up his hands.

He said Purdue all I know is what they told me.

He said I'm the last of the Lewisites and last night I opened all the gas jets in the house.

He said this morning I learned that the gas company had terminated my service two weeks ago.

He said I'm inclined to believe that this may explain the recent soggy condition of my French toast.

I said that's not all.

I said it may have had an adverse effect on your coffee.

5

...you got to look for the sunny side...getting your
toe stepped on ain't no bargain but it beats hell out
of getting kicked in the groin...

Monroe D. Underwood

Suicide Lewisite sat in gloomy silence.

I said so what's on your mind?

I said you didn't come all the way from Radish River just
to step on my toe.

Suicide Lewisite said no I'm here to hire you to
investigate the Radish River Possumcats.

He said we'll pretend you're some kind of sports
reporter and by associating with my players you may be able
to find out what the trouble is.

I said I already know what the trouble is.

I said you got no offense.

I said you also got no defense.

Suicide Lewisite said yes but there must be a reason for this.

He said if it's dissension I got to know about it.

He said this team isn't as bad as it looks and right now I'm angling for the one player who could turn it all around.

He said if I get him we still got a shot at the bacon and I may not commit suicide as soon as expected.

I said if he's that good why isn't he in the National Football League?

Suicide Lewisite said well I understand that he's just a bit on the eccentric side.

He said can you be in Radish River by Saturday?

I said hell I can be in New Zealand by Saturday.

I said I get seventy-five a day.

Suicide Lewisite shook his head.

He said no you don't.

I said who says I don't?

Suicide Lewisite said the new owner of the Possumcats says you don't.

He said the new owner says you get two hundred a day.

He said the new owner seems to think you're worth it.

He said you see this is all the new owner's idea.

He said except the part where I stepped on your toe.

I said who's the new owner?

Suicide Lewisite said some real nice old lady by the name of Hepzibah Dodd.

6

...money will buy anything that ain't important and
a few things that is...beer for one...

Monroe D. Underwood

It was three ayem.

I sat at the dinette table with Betsy.

Betsy was tight-lipped and her big pale-blue eyes
sparkled with fury.

And tears.

She refilled our coffee cups and held a trembling match
for our cigarettes.

She said well it was certainly nice while it lasted.

She said we damn near got back on a first-name basis.

She said isn't that right Joseph?

I shrugged.

I said anything you say Mary.

Betsy said I'm beginning to feel like a goddam orphan.

I said Betsy we need money.

I said the seventy-five I made today was the first buck I've earned since June.

Betsy said well where the hell's the pressure?

She said we still have four thousand in the bank.

I said four grand won't get us around the corner.

Betsy said look why don't I just go to work and put us on easy street?

She said I can be back in business in a week.

She said I'll do it if you'll just stay home and work jigsaw puzzles.

There was a very long silence.

Betsy said Chance I'm sorry about that.

I said Betsy you ought to be.

Betsy said please forget I said it.

I said forget you said what?

Betsy said how long will you be gone this time?

I shrugged.

I said just long enough to locate the trouble with this Radish River football team.

Betsy said that doesn't tell me much.

I said it tells you all I'm able to tell you.

Betsy said I don't understand.

She said a professional football coach drives clear across the state and hires a private detective to find out why his team isn't winning.

She said it simply doesn't rhyme.

She said especially where you're concerned.

She said you don't know a football from a watermelon.

I said the hell I don't.

I said footballs ain't green and watermelons don't got laces.

I said any more coffee?

Betsy poured half-cups.

She was calming down.

I fished another flattened-out Camel from my bathrobe pocket and got it in operation.

Betsy said there's something screwy about this case.

I said Betsy I've never worked a case that wasn't screwy.

Betsy said well my God Chance look where you've been recently.

She said Stranger City and Waupuwukee Downs.

She said look where you're going.

She said Radish River.

She said screwy places screwy cases.

I shrugged.

I said well Betsy I got to make a living.

Betsy said sweetheart let's not fight.

She said you look so tired tonight.

She said did you have a rough day?

I shrugged.

I said well the morning was slow but the afternoon wore me out.

7

...of all the lies that man has lied
The worst is, "God is on our side."...

Monroe D. Underwood

The morning bus to Radish River was crowded and smoky.

It lurched southward on narrow roads winding through the circus hues of young autumn.

We made numerous crossroads stops.

Eventually we picked up a sedate sandy-haired bespectacled gentleman who carried an enormous white-leather Bible.

It had gilt-edged pages and a gold cross on its front.

He paid his fare and looked for a seat.

He had two choices.

Next to a fat woman who had launched an audible all-out attack on a huge red apple.

Or next to me.

He sat next to me.

A mile out of Radish River he said hallelujah!

I didn't say anything.

That stopped him stone cold.

For about ten seconds.

He looked me over.

He said brother have you been washed in the blood?

I shrugged.

I said not really.

I said this suit always looks that way.

There was a half-mile pause.

He said are you going to the game tonight?

I said what game?

He said oh Heavenly Father what do you mean what game?

I said what do you mean oh Heavenly Father what do I mean what game?

I said I'm from Chicago.

He said I refer of course to tonight's football contest between Radish River and Cranberry Creek.

I shrugged.

I said well from what I hear Radish River doesn't have much to holler about.

He said it's the coaching.

He said Suicide Lewisite couldn't coach cows to eat corn.

His hands had begun to tremble slightly.

His eyes had grown hot.

His voice shook.

He raised a bony forefinger.

He said but God is on our side!

He said triumph will be ours in the final accounting!

He said we will shred their unholy carcasses!

He said we shall savor the sweet fruits of victory!

He hauled out a handkerchief and wiped perspiration from his brow.

He was twitching.

He said in Radish River we take our football very seriously.

8

...if a joke ain't cruel it ain't no joke...

Monroe D. Underwood

The bus paused at a traffic signal on the shady outskirts of
Radish River.

To my right was a vacant lot and a huge sign.

In big black block lettering it read,

> GO YOU RADISH RIVER POSSUMCATS
> KICK THEIR GODDAM TEETH OUT GO
> GO GO TEAR THEIR BALLS OFF KILL
> KILL KILL THREE CHEERS FOR RADISH
> RIVER POSSUMCATS HIP HIP HOORAY HIP
> HIP HOORAY.
> RADISH RIVER CHAMBER OF COMMERCE

I got off the bus in front of the Radish River Drug
Store.

A stocky well-dressed graying man of fifty or so was

waiting for me.

He said Mr. Chance Purdue?

I nodded.

The stocky guy shook my hand.

He said I'm Mayor Bradford Boone.

I said congratulations on your election.

Mayor Boone said that was three years ago.

I said better late than never.

Mayor Boone grabbed my suitcase and escorted me to a black Mercedes-Benz parked across the street.

He said I'm to drive you to the residence of the new owner of the Radish River Possumcats.

He said Hepzibah Dodd will be putting you up during your stay with us.

He said she's a sweet little old lady.

He said I don't really believe you'll be in serious danger of sexual attack.

He laughed wildly.

I didn't.

Mayor Boone cleared his throat.

He said yes well apparently that will take care of the humor department for this afternoon.

He said we've really taken old Hepzibah Dodd to our hearts here in Radish River.

He said of course she has no choice but to get rid of Suicide Lewisite.

He said Suicide Lewisite couldn't coach cats to eat canaries.

I shrugged.

I said maybe he just doesn't have the material.

Mayor Boone said well I suppose he's trying.

He said I understand he's been dickering for the services of a super-star named Zanzibar McStrangle.

He said they say McStrangle can really turn a football game around.

I said the name doesn't ring a bell.

I said what college?

Mayor Boone said I'm not certain but I believe I've heard mention of a Barnum-Bailey.

I shrugged.

I said probably one of those small southern schools.

Mayor Boone said Mr. Purdue I'm told that you're a sportswriter.

I nodded.

I said well.

Mayor Boone said I want you to know that favorable comment concerning the Possumcats will be greatly appreciated.

I nodded.

Again.

I said well.

Again.

Mayor Boone said in Radish River we take our football very seriously.

I said I'm beginning to get that impression.

I said I write for a quarterly sports review so my article won't appear until late December.

Mayor Boone said what's the name of the quarterly sports review?

I said *Quarterly Sports Review.*

Mayor Boone said oh yes the *Quarterly Sports Review.*

A white Cadillac covered with hundreds of brightly

colored streamers pulled away from the curb to lead us past a large red brick building where people threw confetti and hollered and waved.

I smiled and waved back.

I said Mayor Boone I appreciate the welcome but you shouldn't have gone to all this trouble.

Mayor Boone said Mr. Purdue we seem to have become entangled in a wedding procession.

9

...from A to Z ain't bad...it's the getting back that
tires you out...

Monroe D. Underwood

Mayor Bradford Boone wheeled his Mercedes-Benz to the
curb in front of an ancient gray frame house.

He said Hepzibah Dodd bought this place last week.

He said the same way she bought the Possumcats.

He said cash on the barrelhead.

I said is she at home now?

Mayor Boone said yes I left her just a few minutes ago.

He said she was reading *An Inquiry Into the Nature and
Causes of the Wealth of Nations.*

He said by Adam Smith.

He said it's difficult to imagine that saintly old lady
having such a wide range of interests.

He said A to Z.

He said economics to football.

I shrugged.

I said that's only E to F.

I opened the door and got out.

I said well Mayor thanks for the lift.

Mayor Boone said anything to help the Possumcats.

He said anything.

His face was suddenly red.

He said any goddam thing at all.

His knuckles had turned white on the steering wheel.

He said we're gonna tear the opposition limb from gut!

Tears welled in his eyes.

He said we're gonna throw their bloody bones to the dogs!

I said Mayor Boone I can hear you from here just fine.

Mayor Boone lowered his voice.

He cleared his throat.

He wiped tiny flecks of spittle from his chin.

He said in Radish River we take our football very seriously.

I said yes I believe you mentioned that.

I picked up my suitcase and went up the walk to the old gray house.

10

...most of us starts out and ends up in bedrooms...

Monroe D. Underwood

I knocked.

The door opened.

Silently.

I stepped into a hallway.

I dropped my suitcase and waited for my eyes to adjust to the sudden dimness.

The door swung closed.

Just as silently.

I detected the faint scent of lilac.

Brandy Alexander stood to my right.

She wore form-fitting black satin pajamas and black patent leather spike heels.

She slipped into my arms.

Her lilac perfume wafted over me.

I held her close and buried my face in her thick dark

wavy hair.

I ran a hand up and down her back.

Further down than up.

Brandy looked at me.

Her liquid brown eyes were wide.

Her perfect nostrils were flared.

Her voice was soft and husky-sweet.

She said oh Jesus Jonah and Judas Iscariot!

I said you took the words right out of my mouth.

Brandy glued her lips to mine.

After a while she said hi Purdue.

Dreamily.

I shrugged.

I said Brandy you win.

I said where the hell's the bedroom?

Brandy stepped back.

She smiled and shook her head.

She said not now Purdue please.

She said we'll make love after the football game.

I said my God Brandy it'll be six hours before the football game starts.

Brandy said yes and that's just the point.

She said I don't want you leaving for a football game when we're only half through.

11

...the Chicago Cubs made a sports reporter their general manager...one look at the record will show you how much sports reporters knows about sports...

Monroe D. Underwood

The Radish River Possumcats played their home games at the Radish River High School stadium.

The Radish River High School was in the process of collapsing from old age but the stadium was new and sparkling.

It had a seating capacity of approximately fifteen thousand.

There was a glossy macadam track that circled the emerald-green football field.

The vast banks of floodlights would have done credit to any major league park in the country.

There was an ultramodern scoreboard some four stories tall.

It was rigged to fire aerial bombs in celebration of Radish River scores.

If any.

On my way to the locker room I passed a giant sign that read DEATH TO THE INVADERS SHOW NO MERCY SLAUGHTER THE DIRTY NO-GOOD BASTARDS THREE CHEERS FOR RADISH RIVER POSSUMCATS HIP HIP HOORAY HIP HIP HOORAY HIP HIP HOORAY HIP HIP HOORAY.

RADISH RIVER CHAMBER OF COMMERCE

Suicide Lewisite greeted me with a firm handshake.

He introduced me to the team as a reporter for a national sports publication.

One of the players said what's the name of the national sports publication?

I said *National Sports Publication.*

The player said oh yeah the *National Sports Publication.*

The team chaplain's name was Reverend H.F. Brimstone.

Reverend H.F. Brimstone was a tall emaciated man with glaring gray eyes.

He stepped forward to offer the pregame prayer.

He raised his hands.

He said every head bowed and every eye closed please.

In a solemn stentorian voice Reverend H.F. Brimstone said oh Lord of Hosts who delivered Daniel from the lions' den and Shadrach from the fiery furnace not to mention Meshach and Abednego we ask now for Thy greatest miracle which would prevent these Radish River Possumcats from blowing this one by more than forty-nine points repeat Lord forty-nine points.

He said Blessed Redeemer in Thy boundless mercy

see to it that only the minimum be maimed for life and we plead for the souls of those who will most certainly die in the coming hours of black defeat and we pray for the bereaved parents who shall have snatched from them this night their sons and whose doors on the bleak morrow of despair will bear wreaths of sorrow yea sweeten their bitter cups Lord and with these humble requests we send our gallant youngsters forth to be massacred on the gory field of combat Amen.

When every head was raised and every eye was opened it developed that half the Radish River football team was missing.

It also developed that the remaining half refused to take the field.

Suicide Lewisite was on the verge of tears until the locker room telephone rang.

He answered it and broke into a beaming smile.

He crashed the phone back into its cradle.

He said all right fellas let's get the hell out there!

He said Zanzibar McStrangle is on the sidelines waiting to play for good old Radish River!

The Possumcats gave a lusty cheer and charged through the door into the night.

Suicide Lewisite looked at me.

He said you have just heard Reverend H.F. Brimstone's very last prayer for the Radish River Possumcats.

He banged his locker door shut with a vengeance.

He said next week I am replacing that crepe-hanging bastard with a goddam witch doctor.

Before we went out Suicide Lewisite said be careful when we step into the open.

He said in Radish River they take their football very seriously.

He said one of these crackpots brought a squirrel rifle to the opener.

He said he gunned down twenty-two flying footballs before we could get the sonofabitch arrested.

When the crowd saw Suicide Lewisite a great roar went up.

Cantaloupes and tomatoes and aged eggs flew from every direction.

Some people gnashed their teeth and others tore their hair and a great many frothed at the mouth and all of them cursed horribly.

I heard any number of comments regarding the morals of Suicide Lewisite's mother.

There were those in attendance who offered Suicide Lewisite advice on how to conduct his sex life.

The preponderance of this advice had to do with geese.

Galloping geese.

Suicide Lewisite ducked a tomahawk that embedded itself in a goalpost.

He ducked a copy of *An Inquiry Into the Nature and Causes of the Wealth of Nations.*

By Adam Smith.

He ducked an old washing machine motor which someone had neglected to remove from the old washing machine.

He ducked an enormous white-leather Bible with gilt-edged pages and a gold cross on its front.

He said if you think this is something just stick around for the Annual Radish River Roman Chariot Race which is to be held at halftime of next week's game with the Sycamore

Center Ridgelings.

I said how does it work?

Suicide Lewisite said it doesn't.

He said the event is open to any nutty local businessman who can scrounge up a busted-down horse and a makeshift chariot and a bed sheet.

He said last year there was a high wind and three chariot drivers got their sheets blown off.

He said they got arrested for indecent exposure and two of them came down with pneumonia and one of them damn near died and all three of them lost the race and it seems there must be better ways to spend one's time.

He said just the thought of such foolishness makes me want to commit suicide.

He said by comparison even football makes sense.

12

...it costs two cents to grow a head of lettuce and
a quarter to get it picked and fifty cents to ship it
and a man would starve to death on it in a week...

Monroe D. Underwood

Zanzibar McStrangle stood near the Radish River bench.

He munched a head of lettuce.

He surveyed the scene with the impassivity of the
seasoned professional.

He was probably no taller than five-three but he must
have weighed close to five hundred pounds.

He had a dark pugnacious face and quick beady eyes and
great hairy hands.

In his Radish River football uniform of Lombardy
lavender and peachy cream he was indeed a sight to behold.

Suicide Lewisite assembled his squad and announced that
Zanzibar McStrangle would play tackle on defense and that he
would operate as number-one running back on offense.

The Cranberry Creek Gobblers won the coin-toss and elected to receive.

They returned the kickoff to the fifty.

Their first play from scrimmage went right up the middle.

Zanzibar McStrangle seized a Cranberry Creek lineman.

He held him high in the air with one hand.

He brought him down on the unfortunate Cranberry Creek ball carrier with a resounding thud that drove the poor bastard six inches into the turf.

The Radish River fans went wild with joy.

Suicide Lewisite was grinning from ear to ear.

The Cranberry Creek Gobblers decided to pass.

Their quarterback dropped into the pocket and looked for a receiver.

Zanzibar McStrangle rumbled into the Cranberry Creek backfield like a bulldozer into an anthill.

The quarterback retreated.

Zanzibar McStrangle caught him in the parking lot across the street.

He was attempting to stuff the hysterical athlete into the gas tank of a Radish River school bus when Suicide Lewisite arrived in the nick of time with a case of bananas.

At the close of the first half Radish River led Cranberry Creek 359-0.

The night had been blown to smithereens by an incessant scoreboard barrage of aerial bombs.

359-0 proved to be the final score.

The Cranberry Creek Gobblers failed to return for the second half kickoff.

I heard later that a few had entered monasteries

and that the remainder had bought guitars to become wandering minstrels.

The Radish River fans held a torchlight parade that went on until three o'clock Sunday afternoon.

In Radish River they take their football very seriously.

13

...there is only three creatures what laughs...loons
and hyenas and humans...of these loons is the
least offensive...

Monroe D. Underwood

Brandy Alexander sat naked and cross-legged on the bed
with her chin cupped in the palm of one hand.

She had been studying me for some time.

At last she shook her head.

She said Purdue why is it I never tire of you?

I shrugged.

Brandy said oooooh wow!

She said encore encore encore!

I said baby if you get an encore it'll be with mirrors.

Brandy said not sex Purdue.

She said the shrug.

She said shrug for me.

I said I just did.

Brandy said I mean again.

I said aw come on Brandy.

I said any damn fool can shrug.

Brandy said yes but not like you Purdue.

She said please?

I shrugged.

Brandy said oh my God that just drives me nuts!

She said it's so damned sexy!

She threw herself on top of me.

She put her lips close to mine.

She said one more time Purdue.

I said Brandy one of us is crazy and I got a hunch it doesn't stop there.

I dozed off to the sound of Brandy's musical laughter.

It was a nice sound to doze off to.

14

...Don Quixote was a guy what went around
pretending he was something he wasn't...started
an irreversible trend...

Monroe D. Underwood

Sunday morning across the table from an unclothed Brandy
Alexander is an experience not easily dismissed.

My coffee had gone stone cold before I remembered I
had it.

Brandy wrinkled her flawless nose at me.

She said is something wrong?

I said not that I can think of.

Brandy said then what are you staring at?

I shrugged.

Brandy said whatever it is it must be mighty damned
interesting.

She said your eyes are crossed.

I said well in the first place it isn't an it.

I said it's a them.

I said and in the second place I didn't start it.

I said they stared at me first.

Brandy said shall I put on a brassiere?

I said I didn't say that.

Brandy lit two cigarettes and handed one to me.

She said Purdue I suppose you're looking for answers.

I chuckled.

I said well by God Brandy I simply can't imagine what the hell ever gave you that idea.

I said all that's happening is you're galloping around impersonating the widow of Don Quixote and making screwball telephone calls and buying football teams ten miles from where Christ lost his moccasins and dragging me into hick towns to pose as what I ain't in order that I can do something I don't have the slightest goddam idea how to do so why should I want answers?

Brandy shook her head and sighed.

She pushed her coffee cup to one side.

She folded her arms on the table.

She leaned forward and looked at me intently.

She said Purdue I adopted the role of Hepzibah Dodd when I realized that I was being followed and that my office and apartment telephones were tapped.

She said somebody knows that I'm onto something important.

She said Hepzibah Dodd gave me freedom of movement and pay telephones provided me with a certain amount of privacy.

She said the CIA arranged my temporary possession of an apartment above the Fall Out Inn.

She said I occupied it as Hepzibah Dodd and I contacted you as Mrs. Jonesberry.

I said why didn't you just call and say you wanted to see me?

I said the phone at Wallace's Tavern isn't bugged.

Brandy said I wanted to test my disguise.

She said I figured that if a man who knew every inch of me couldn't crack it no one could.

I said where does the CIA come in?

Brandy said the CIA is picking up the tab for the entire operation.

She said the football team and this house and both of our paychecks.

She said I brought you down here on a couple of ridiculous pretexts and here we are in Radish River with ideal cover for our activities.

She said I'm an eccentric old bat who bought a minor league football team for a plaything and you're the guy she hired as her legman.

I said where did Hepzibah Dodd sit at the game last night?

Brandy said in the east end-zone seats.

She said near the locker room doors.

I said did she throw that copy of *An Inquiry Into the Nature and Causes of the Wealth of Nations?*

I said by Adam Smith?

Brandy said yes it was an excellent opportunity to get rid of the damned thing.

She said it's been a valuable prop but Hepzibah was tired of carrying it around.

She said besides the fans just loved it.

I said okay so now we're in Radish River fooling everybody.

I said especially me.

I said why?

Brandy said I won't go into that just yet.

She said but I can tell you that this is by far the biggest damned thing you and I have ever tackled.

I shrugged.

Brandy said there's strong evidence indicating that Radish River has been selected as the point of emergence.

I said as the what?

Brandy said point of emergence.

I said well I will be eternally doodledy-ding-donged.

Brandy said Purdue when you learn what I'm talking about you won't take it so lightly.

I said so who's taking it lightly?

I said I just realized I'm down to one cigarette.

15

...these days if you ain't crazy you just got to be eccentric...

Monroe D. Underwood

I walked northward up the narrow sidewalk toward the tiny business district of Radish River.

I came to a small grassy park.

I paused and smoked my last beat-up cigarette before continuing on to the Radish River Drug Store.

I bought a carton of busted Camels.

On my way out I spotted Suicide Lewisite seated at the soda fountain.

He was pouring a Super-Kola into an enormous self-satisfied smile.

He said good-morning Purdue.

He said I am so happy I could commit suicide.

I said I wish to make a report.

Suicide Lewisite slapped me on the back.

He said way to go in there Purdue.

He said what do you wish to report?

I said I wish to report that Zanzibar McStrangle is a gorilla.

Suicide Lewisite choked on his Super-Kola.

He said crazy talk always makes me want to commit suicide.

I said I have just been watching Zanzibar McStrangle in the park.

I said he is swinging from tree to tree.

I said he is beating his chest and carrying on in a most gorillalike manner.

Suicide Lewisite said look Purdue I told you that McStrangle is a trifle eccentric.

He said once in a while he gets the idea that he is the Scarlet Pimpernel.

He said at other times he pretends he is Flash Gordon.

He said now and then it's Tarzan.

He said this morning it just happens to be Tarzan.

I said oh.

Suicide Lewisite said do you have anything else to report?

I said one other item.

I said he's still wearing his football uniform.

16

...if we eliminated all the other months we'd have
one hell of a long September...

Monroe D. Underwood

On Sunday evening there was a big football rally in the little
grassy park.

The Radish River High School band played "Go You
Possumcats" and "Bust Their Rotten Asses Radish River."

When the crowd sang "Lombardy Lavender and Peachy
Cream Forever" there wasn't a dry eye in the park.

Zanzibar McStrangle was made an honorary lifetime
citizen of Radish River.

He was given a standing ovation.

He responded by flinging a chair into the top branches
of an oak tree.

The fact that the chair was occupied by Mayor Bradford
Boone failed to dampen the crowd's enthusiasm.

When the rally was over I walked slowly toward

Brandy's house.

An autumn moon rode high above Radish River and there was a distant smell of burning leaves and I got that September feeling.

I tried to remember when I had first realized that Old Man Time was on my trail.

I couldn't pinpoint it but I was sure of one thing.

It had happened about the time I met Brandy Alexander.

17

...a briefcase is something what is carried by a
guy what don't want the neighbors to know he is a
janitor...

Monroe D. Underwood

There was a long dark automobile parked in Brandy
Alexander's driveway.

As I approached I saw a tall slender man leave the car.

He had a briefcase.

He carried it to Brandy's front porch and placed it inside
the screen door.

He started back to the car.

That was all I needed.

I'd seen the routine in the movies.

He planted a bomb.

I broke into a gallop.

I cut him off a couple of steps short of his automobile.

I hit him very hard on the jaw.

He fell backward.

Like a tree.

A redwood tree.

I heard Brandy's front door open.

Brandy's voice was guardedly subdued.

She said Sir Lennox?

I said nope.

I said Purdue.

Brandy said oh.

She said have you met Sir Lennox?

I said the name fails to ring a bell.

Brandy came down from the front porch.

She was wearing her brown robe.

She looked at the prostrate man.

She threw her hands to her face.

She said oh my God.

She said Purdue you've just coldcocked Sir Lennox Nilgood Fiddleduck of Scotland Yard.

I said oh yeah?

I said what's in that goddam briefcase?

Brandy said vibrations-monitoring information.

I shrugged.

I said hell nobody ever tells me anything.

18

...television is something what is built by the least-paid for the least-intelligent...

Monroe D. Underwood

Sir Lennox Nilgood Fiddleduck was an angular darkly handsome man with a deeply resonant voice.

He sat drinking a steaming cup of tea and rubbing his jaw.

I said sorry Sir Lennox.

Sir Lennox grinned a rueful grin.

He said good show Purdue.

He glanced at Brandy.

He said I'm bloody glad he's on our side.

Brandy said yes wouldn't that be nice?

She said Purdue will it be all right if I run into the bedroom to dress?

She said I mean you won't hit Sir Lennox on the head with a piano or anything like that?

I shrugged.

I said you ain't even got no goddam piano.

Brandy came over and kissed me on the cheek.

She whispered Purdue don't be sore.

I shrugged.

Brandy excused herself and left the room.

Sir Lennox produced an old briar pipe.

He loaded it with coarse dark tobacco.

He put a match to it.

It smelled like a six-alarm junkyard fire.

Sir Lennox leaned back and smiled.

He said well Purdue the game is afoot.

I didn't say anything.

Sir Lennox said the infamous Doctor Ho Ho Ho is up to his old tricks.

He said he's a Chinese fiend incarnate.

He said he has the intellect of an Einstein and the outlook of a bloody king cobra.

He said he loves to kill and there's no limit to his bizarre methods of eradicating human life.

He said in London he tricked one of our best operatives into visiting a WCTU meeting shortly after the Super-Kola had been spiked with Spanish fly.

He paled at the recollection.

He wiped away a tear.

He said good old Reggie.

He said in New York he lashed one of your FBI men to a chair in front of a television set.

He said the poor blighter laughed himself to death.

I felt a ripple of cold horror run up my spine.

I said oh good Lord man don't tell me he was forced to

watch the 1972 Democratic National Convention.

Sir Lennox nodded.

His voice broke.

He said every blooming minute of it.

Both of us shuddered.

I said frankly I believe our best television programs to be the test patterns.

Sir Lennox said oh veddy true and you Yanks have cornered the humorous test-pattern market.

I said I like those patterns with the different colored lines.

Sir Lennox smiled broadly.

He said oh yes by Jove those are smashers.

I said have you ever seen the one with the big circle and that goofy-looking Indian?

Sir Lennox said oh ripping simply ripping.

He threw back his head and roared with merriment for several minutes.

He caught his breath and wiped his eyes.

He said blimey matey I had nearly forgotten that one.

He said my favorite is the one with all those bloody little squares.

He slapped his knee and laughed until his face was red.

He was still in stitches when Brandy returned.

Brandy said I don't know what you boys have been drinking but I'll have a gallon on the rocks.

At this Sir Lennox let out a wild whoop and fell to his knees doubled-over in convulsions of laughter.

Brandy looked at me.

Blankly.

She said I can see it now.

She said my name up in lights.

She said Brandy Alexander the Broadway Sunbeam Girl.
She did a little sideways dance step.
She said twenty-three-ski-goddam-doo.
She flopped into a chair.
She said shit.

19

...a man can get sicker on wine than just about anything...this also holds true for women...

Monroe D. Underwood

I was puffing.

Heavily.

Brandy was panting.

Softly.

Her head was on my shoulder and her lilac perfume was scrambling my senses.

Her cigarette glowed ruby-red in the darkness.

She said Purdue you improve with age.

She said like quality wine.

I said I really ain't too much on wine.

Brandy said you're more mellow than when we first met.

I said I drink beer mostly.

Brandy said you're wonderfully robust but smooth as silk.

I said of course I'll drink whiskey on occasion.

Brandy said you're strong but you're gentle and just sweet enough.

I said just about any occasion come to think of it.

Brandy snubbed out her cigarette.

She rolled over and snuggled up tight.

She put her lips to my ear.

Her voice was soft.

She said Purdue?

I said yeah?

Brandy said Purdue please shut up.

20

...if you was to put all the Chinamen in one room
you would need a rather large room...

Monroe D. Underwood

I was sitting on the edge of the bed rubbing my eyes.

Brandy came to the bedroom door.

She said my God I thought you were in hibernation.

I said no but we stopped there on a troop train once.

Brandy said it's after ten o'clock.

I said it's about fifty miles out of Ashtabula.

Brandy said do you want breakfast?

I said after that we didn't stop all night.

Brandy said the coffee's ready.

I said except to take water.

Brandy sighed.

I said I think it was for water.

Brandy went away.

I dressed and stumbled into the kitchen.

I fired up a battered Camel and sat across from Brandy.

She was wearing her brown robe.

Closed tightly at the throat.

I said no double feature this morning?

Brandy shook her head.

She said not this morning.

She said I want you to concentrate on what I have to say.

I shrugged.

Neither of us spoke until Brandy poured my second cup of coffee.

She said I think you should know that this could be damned dangerous.

I said why?

I said the first cup was fine.

Brandy said now Purdue don't start up with me again.

She said you know perfectly well what I'm talking about.

She said Doctor Ho Ho Ho is the most savage and merciless creature in all of history.

She said you still have time to get out.

I said if it's all the same to you I'd like to wait and see the Annual Radish River Roman Chariot Race.

Brandy said is that the only reason?

I shrugged.

Brandy looked at me with level liquid brown eyes.

She said Purdue I know you love me.

I said is that a question?

Brandy said of course not.

I said then I don't have to answer it.

Brandy said don't you dare.

I said tell me about Doctor Ho Ho Ho.

Brandy said Sir Lennox Nilgood Fiddleduck had a brush with Doctor Ho Ho Ho years ago.

She said at that time Ho Ho Ho was plotting to blow up Buckingham Palace.

She said strictly bush-league when compared to what he has in mind this time around.

I said I'll bite.

Brandy stared into her coffee cup.

Her voice grew solemn.

She said Purdue he's about to invade the United States of America.

I said then what are we doing in southern Illinois?

I said we should be on the West Coast.

I said or the East Coast.

I said or some goddam coast.

Brandy shook her head.

She said he won't invade by sea.

I said paratroopers?

Brandy said no.

I said well those are the only ways you can get here from there.

Brandy said you missed one.

She said Doctor Ho Ho Ho is digging a hole straight through the earth from the Russian side of the Manchurian border.

She said if our calculations are correct he'll emerge in the Radish River area within a week.

She said Sir Lennox is in charge of our monitoring

facilities and his recent readings have put Ho Ho Ho well east of the Missouri border.

I said this Ho Ho Ho must be a real bastard with a shovel.

Brandy said Purdue he's using the most sophisticated drilling equipment ever designed.

She said the operation has occupied thousands of people.

I said I thought we were getting on better terms with the Chinese.

Brandy nodded.

She said we are.

She said if Ho Ho Ho shows up in China they'll hang him so high he'll freeze to death before he runs out of breath.

I said does the Russian government approve of this kind of carrying on?

Brandy said well Purdue that takes us right back to square one.

She said we're up against DADA again.

I said are those maniacs still running around loose?

Brandy said the DADA organization has been recalled to Mother Russia explicitly for the Ho Ho Ho program.

She said they've worked with Ho Ho Ho every inch of the way.

She said DADA even designed the uniforms for Ho Ho Ho's forces.

She said bright red with white helmets.

She said very sharp.

She said DADA arranged for Ho Ho Ho to break ground in a Russian-occupied Manchurian area that the

Chinese have claimed for years.

She said this enables the Kremlin to look on without saying yes or no.

I said the Kremlin wouldn't say yes or no.

Brandy said once Ho Ho Ho's troops begin to surface they'll come boiling out of that hole at a rate of fifty thousand a day.

I said the Kremlin would say *da* or *nyet*.

She said if Ho Ho Ho can escape notice for a few days he'll have half a million troops in the center of America with more pouring in by the minute.

I said the reason I know about *da* and *nyet* is I got a phonetic Russian dictionary at home.

Brandy said Purdue stop it.

I said that must be one helluva hole.

Brandy said yes to be perfectly honest it's the foremost engineering feat in the history of mankind.

She said still it hasn't been as difficult as it would have been to tunnel from say Ecuador to Borneo.

I said safer too.

I said no wild men.

Brandy winced.

She said all right Purdue that does it.

She stood and pulled the belt of her brown robe.

She wiggled her tawny smooth shoulders.

The robe rustled to the floor.

Brandy took my hand.

She said come with me.

On our way into the bedroom she said how do you say this in Russian wise guy?

I shrugged.

I said well somebody knows.

I said all those goddam Russians didn't get here by accident.

THE RADISH RIVER CAPER

21

...big advantage about living forever is you might see the Cubs win a World Series...

Monroe D. Underwood

Later when we were tired I said what does this Doctor Ho Ho Ho look like?

Brandy said nobody has the remotest idea.

I said well at least we know he's Chinese.

Brandy said no we don't.

She said Sir Lennox is operating on that theory but it's mere supposition.

She said we know where Ho Ho Ho has been and we know what he's done but we have little else to go on.

She said it's been rumored that Ho Ho Ho has perfected an age-retarding process and that he wears leopard-skin shorts and that he speaks eighty-nine different languages including twenty-two that he made up himself and that he has direct pipelines into the offices of every government on earth and that he sang bass in a barbershop quartet in Bartlett Illinois ten years ago.

I shrugged.

I said well you can throw that last one out.

I said I've been in Bartlett Illinois.

I said Bartlett Illinois didn't have a barbershop ten years ago.

22

...being minus a plus ain't quite as bad as being plus a minus but you still don't got much to write home about...

Monroe D. Underwood

Smiling September brings bittersweet tears.

All songs are sad songs.

Dreams drift away to wherever dreams drift away to and I got a pebble in my sock as I passed the grassy little park.

I sat on a bench with the sun warm on my back.

I removed the pebble.

I smoked a couple dilapidated Camels.

I blew tobacco smoke into the blue autumn haze.

I opened the vault of my life in search of a plus or two.

That was a mistake.

I got flattened by an avalanche of minuses.

Well there was nothing mysterious about it.

Some dirty bastard had reversed my escalator.

With me smack-dab in the middle.

I was the guy who went out to lock the barn after the horse had been stolen.

And found the barn missing.

Nowhere to go and no way to get there.

I shrugged.

Another fifty years and it wouldn't matter.

The thump of a bass drum and the sound of voices drifted into my thinking.

A group of people entered the park.

They bore aloft a huge banner which read ZANZIBAR McSTRANGLE FOR PRESIDENT.

From across the park came the rat-a-tat-tat of a snare drum.

Another group of people appeared.

This group carried small signs.

KEEP ZANZIBAR McSTRANGLE PURE.

SAVE ZANZIBAR McSTRANGLE FROM THE POLITICAL JUNGLE.

ZANZIBAR McSTRANGLE IS A FULLBACK NOT A ½ WIT.

The opposing factions met in the middle of the park.

Words were exchanged.

Fists were shaken.

There was an excellent riot.

Nineteen people went to jail and I went to the Radish River Drug Store.

I called Betsy.

Betsy said hello my sweetheart when are you coming home to mama?

I shrugged.

I said probably right after Doctor Ho Ho Ho invades the United States.

There was a lengthy period of silence.

Betsy said I see.

She said will that be before or after the cow jumps over the moon?

I said apparently it will be right about the time the Radish River Possumcats play the Sycamore Center Ridgelings.

Betsy said what's a ridgeling?

I said it's a horse with only one testicle.

Betsy said then what do you call a horse with three testicles?

I said well I knew a guy who had a horse with three testicles.

I said he called it Blackie.

Betsy hung up.

Mayor Bradford Boone was entering the drugstore.

He had a bad limp.

I said did you get that limp from falling out of the oak tree?

Mayor Boone said no I got it from Suicide Lewisite stepping on my toe.

He said Purdue would you believe they blew off seven tons of aerial bombs Saturday night?

He said they loaded another fifteen tons into the scoreboard this morning.

He said they figure they can shoot up the whole bunch if Zanzibar McStrangle plays up to his potential this weekend.

I shrugged.
Betsy had summed it up.
Crazy places crazy cases.

23

...speaking of atrocities...has you ever seen what
the Chicago White Sox can do to a fly ball?...

Monroe D. Underwood

From the dim depths of a Tuesday night cloud of pipe
smoke Sir Lennox Nilgood Fiddleduck said it appears
certain that the evil Chinaman will reach Radish River in
four or five days.

He said history indicates that Sunday will be the big
day.

He said the Japanese did veddy well against you chaps
on a Sunday.

I shrugged.

I said well that would depend on just what Sunday you're
talking about.

I said if it's Sunday December 7th you're right.

I said if it's Sunday September 2nd you're wrong.

Brandy said just where do you figure Doctor Ho Ho Ho

will emerge?

Sir Lennox ran his pipe stem across the big map on Brandy's kitchen table.

He tapped confidently on a darkened area.

He said right here in Gunther's Woods just west of the Radish River city limits.

He said Gunther's Woods is large and dense and it offers excellent cover for an operation of this magnitude.

Brandy shook her head emphatically.

She said no.

Sir Lennox frowned.

He said but it's far and away the most likely spot.

Brandy said yes and that's why Ho Ho Ho won't use it.

I said when will the Marines arrive?

Brandy said they won't.

I said well then the Army?

Brandy said the Army won't be here either.

I said well how about the Air Force or the Knights of Columbus or maybe Alcoholics Anonymous?

I said we got us a national emergency don't we?

Brandy said Purdue we're completely on our own in Radish River.

She said Washington doesn't want to risk an involvement.

I said hold it right there.

I said what do you mean Washington doesn't want to risk an involvement?

I said Jesus Christ the country is about to be goddam invaded.

I said ain't that worth an involvement?

Brandy said Purdue stop shouting and try to be realistic.

She said if American troops were to injure one of Doctor Ho Ho Ho's men the American Civil Liberties Union would have our Joint Chiefs of Staff over a barrel in ten minutes.

She said then our news media would start screaming atrocity atrocity atrocity.

She said within twenty-four hours our students would be demonstrating from coast to coast.

She said you simply have to understand that there isn't so much as a single sliver of American backbone left in Washington D.C.

She said nobody will stand up to be counted.

She said even the financing of this venture is under the table.

She said if we attract the slightest amount of unfavorable attention here in Radish River the CIA won't admit it's ever heard of us.

She said what's more both of us will probably get life imprisonment.

I said what the hell for?

I said my God all we did was go to a football game.

I said half of that couldn't be played.

Brandy said all Nixon did was make a few tape recordings.

She said half of those couldn't be played either.

I said well I'll be a dirty sonofabitch.

Sir Lennox said pardon me but isn't that what General Skinny Wainwright said on Luzon in 1942?

I said look you just got to get your dates straightened

out.

I said that's what General Hideki Tojo said in Tokyo in 1945.

24

...there ain't no truth in the report that I live in a haunted house...that was only my mother-in-law looking out the window...

Monroe D. Underwood

Radish River moonlight flooded Brandy's spavined old front porch.

I sat on the second step.

Brandy occupied the fourth.

It was a warm quiet night and very late.

Brandy sat with her elbows on her knees and her chin in her hands.

She smiled down at me.

Her soft husky-sweet voice was sentimental.

She said Purdue this is like when I was a kid.

She said don't you get that impression?

I shrugged.

Just a left shoulder shrug.

I said I don't know what it was like when you were a kid.

Brandy said I mean sitting and talking on the front porch steps after dark.

I said we didn't have a front porch.

I said my old man sold it.

Brandy said well somebody in your neighborhood must have had a front porch.

I thought about it.

I said yeah the Cummings family.

I said we used to sit and talk on the steps after dark.

Brandy said did you really?

Down the block a yellowish streetlight flickered weakly.

Leaves rustled in the night.

I said we used to tell ghost stories.

Brandy said I'll bet that was fun.

She said did you have a girlfriend?

I shrugged.

Right shoulder.

I said well sort of.

I said Mary Ann Cummings.

I said she used to loan me her bike.

I said I wrecked it once.

I said as a matter of fact I wrecked it three times.

Brandy said Mary Ann Cummings must have really liked you.

I didn't say anything.

Neither did Brandy.

She was staring into the darkness.

I said didn't you ever tell ghost stories when you were a kid?

Brandy leaned forward and put a hand on my shoulder.

She spoke in a shuttered voice.

She said Purdue there's somebody out there in the trees.

I grinned.

Brandy said I'm sure of it.

I said that's the idea.

Brandy said two of them.

I said spooky stuff.

Brandy said Purdue dammit listen to me.

She said when I count to three hit the ground and roll.

I said hey that's the spirit.

I chuckled.

I said get it?

I said spirit?

Brandy said oh God.

I said don't forget the Holy Ghost.

I laughed.

I said get it?

I said ghost?

Brandy could kick like a mule.

I hit the cracked concrete walk on the back of my neck.

Brandy landed beside me.

She said now roll!

I rolled.

Brandy said oh Lord have mercy.

She said not this direction Purdue.

She said the other direction.

I said well you should have said left or right.

Brandy said merciful Christ do you think it would have helped?

I said hell it would have been worth a try.

Brandy swore.

She said Purdue just forget it and get off of me.

I said Brandy this wasn't my idea in the first place.

Brandy's liquid brown eyes were blistering me.

She said look.

She said the position is acceptable but the location is nothing short of abominable.

I shrugged.

Both shoulders.

Brandy said stop shrugging.

She said people could get the wrong impression.

I said don't worry about it.

I said they're gone.

Brandy said who for Christ's sake?

I shrugged.

I said just a couple guys with long pieces of pipe.

I said they ran down the street.

Brandy said get off you big bastard.

I stood and helped her to her feet.

Brandy dusted herself off.

She said I guess it's all right now.

I said well guess again.

I said you shouldn't go around kicking people down the stairs.

I said I never kick you down the stairs.

I said how would you like it if I kicked you down the stairs?

Brandy said Purdue shut up.

She said that's an order.

She said just shut up and look at the porch.

I looked at the porch.

Stuck in the second and fourth steps were two tiny darts.

Brandy dislodged them.

She said blow-gun size.

She said there's no point in having them analyzed.

She said they'll be loaded to the scuppers with strychnos curare.

I shrugged.

I said Brandy you can kick me down the stairs any old time.

Brandy said well Purdue we've learned one thing.

She said Doctor Ho Ho Ho's advance party is in town.

I said make it two things.

Brandy nodded.

She said I know.

She said our cover isn't as good as we thought it was.

25

... if you smile at Cleveland stay the hell out of Chicago... you might laugh yourself to death ...

Monroe D. Underwood

It was well after three in the morning.

I was trying to get my wind back.

I said Brandy you could wipe out the whole damn Light Brigade.

Brandy said once more unto the breach dear friend?

I said not just yet kiddo.

Brandy's laugh was soft in the darkness.

She stroked my chest.

She said Purdue who's the best woman you've ever been in bed with?

I shrugged.

I said probably a girl who was training to be a missionary.

Brandy said I don't mean that kind of best.

She said I'm talking about performance only.

I shrugged.

I said either Betsy or you.

I said you're both incredible.

I said you're probably a little more incredible than Betsy.

I said at least right now.

Brandy said do you miss Betsy?

I said not when I'm with you.

Brandy said do you ever miss me?

I said not when I'm with Betsy.

Brandy said the team at bat always wins?

I shrugged.

I said something like that.

Brandy said Purdue you'd make a rotten umpire.

I said why bother?

I said I'm already a rotten private detective.

After a long time Brandy said Purdue?

I said yeah?

Brandy said tell me about the girl who was training to be a missionary.

I shrugged.

I said there isn't much to tell.

Brandy said did she become a missionary?

I said not for long.

Brandy said why?

I said she quit.

Brandy said did she like sex that well?

I said sex had nothing to do with it.

I said they sent her to Cleveland.

Brandy said oh dear God in Heaven.
I said that's what she said.

26

*...if the next move ain't the right move it might be
the last move...*

Monroe D. Underwood

Brandy lit a brace of cigarettes and put one in my mouth.

She said well there's very little that can be done about it.

She said Doctor Ho Ho Ho has our number and that's all there is to it.

I shrugged.

I said well I didn't really believe that those poisoned darts came from General Motors.

Brandy said we're between a rock and a hard place.

She shook her head.

She said fifty thousand troops a day.

She said I don't like the odds.

She said any ideas?

I shrugged.

I said sure.

I said if you can get 'em all in bed we got a chance.

Brandy said we'll have to hit them the very moment they show.

She said furthermore we have to make it look like an accident.

She said if only we knew where they'll come up.

I said Fiddleduck is dead set on Gunther's Woods.

Brandy's laugh was impatiently sharp.

She said absolutely not.

She said Ho Ho Ho knows we're onto him.

She said if we weren't onto him we wouldn't be in Radish River.

She said Gunther's Woods is ideal for Ho Ho Ho's purposes.

She said Ho Ho Ho knows it and he knows that we know it.

She said forget about Gunther's Woods.

I shrugged.

I said what's our next move?

Brandy said at the moment we don't have one.

She said we'll just have to continue going through the motions.

She said I'll carry on as Hepzibah Dodd and you'll have to report to Suicide Lewisite now and then.

She said any damn fool kind of report will suffice.

She said we still have a little time to outfox this diabolical monster.

She crushed her cigarette into the ashtray.

She said damned little.

She reached for me.

She said let's make the most of it.

27

...leap frog is a game what has been played by just about everybody but frogs...

Monroe D. Underwood

On the next afternoon Suicide Lewisite occupied a fifty-yard-line seat high in the nearly empty Radish River High School stadium.

The only activity was at the scoreboard where a big black truck unloaded boxes.

Suicide Lewisite stared down at the scene of his magnificent Saturday night triumph.

A slight smile toyed with one corner of his mouth.

He said I guess they thought we should lay in a few more tons of aerial bombs just in case the Possumcats run hog wild against Sycamore Center.

I shrugged and sat down beside him.

He looked at me from the corner of his eye.

He said Purdue I hope you haven't brought me any

more goofy gorilla stories.

I said no but I'm here to make a report.

I said I ran into some of your players at the drugstore earlier in the day.

I said they're certainly an amiable bunch.

I said I saw absolutely no signs of the dissension that seemed to concern you.

I said they just sat at the soda fountain and laughed ha-ha-ha and har-de-har-har-har.

I said one was laughing tee-hee-hee.

Suicide Lewisite said which one was laughing tee-hee-hee?

I said I forget.

Suicide Lewisite said well try to remember because I am going to throw him off the team.

I said they told naughty stories and they sang "We'll Be Standing 'Neath the Streetlight at Ten on Friday Night Singing Songs of Love in Harmony."

Suicide Lewisite frowned.

He said well the words are catchy but what the hell's the name of the song?

I said I learned a few things that might be of interest to you.

Suicide Lewisite said such as?

I said such as Slippery Sleighballs has some sort of mental block because he was conceived during a leapfrog contest at a Southern Baptist picnic.

Suicide Lewisite yawned.

He said is that right?

I said yeah in the boathouse.

I said the janitor and the preacher's wife.

I said the janitor was drowned later.

I said while the preacher was baptizing him.

Suicide Lewisite nodded.

He said you got more such goodies?

I said Barracuda Barinelli dropped out of school when he was sixteen.

Suicide Lewisite said yes I have always assumed as much.

He said probably from a third story window.

He said on his head.

He said in a rock pile.

He said what else?

I said well there's Half-Yard Blunderfoot.

Suicide Lewisite said what about him?

I said he seems well adjusted but he has an unusual hobby.

I said he spends the off-season painting wild animals.

Suicide Lewisite said well he better be careful not to get turpentine on their rear ends.

He said particularly them goddam mountain lions.

28

...the Devil won't take the hindmosts...Hell is already full of foremosts...

Monroe D. Underwood

We leaned against the iron railing that skirted the top of the stadium.

Suicide Lewisite watched the late afternoon sun flame low over the distant vast green expanses of Gunther's Woods.

He said we got a sellout for the Sycamore Center game.

He said when we win this one we'll be right back in the race.

He placed one foot on the bottom rung of the railing.

A faraway look came into his eyes.

He said you know Purdue football is a strange business.

He said there are times when it seems that true quality will never be appreciated.

He said no more than a week ago I was afraid to come out of the house on a clear day.

He said people spat at me.

He said they set their dogs on me.

He said children stoned me in the streets.

He slapped his knee with the flat of his hand.

He said it all changed after we played Cranberry Creek.

He said immediately following the game a sedate sandy-haired bespectacled guy ran up and hollered hallelujah and told me that the true mark of greatness was on me just like it was on King David in the Bible.

He said the Radish River Chamber of Commerce told me that I'm better than Stagg and Bryant and Hayes all put together.

He said just this morning Mayor Bradford Boone said that I'm certain to be approached by every franchise in the whole damn National Football League.

He said hell the gas company even turned my gas back on.

I shrugged.

I said well that's nice.

I said let's just hope that Zanzibar McStrangle stays on the tracks.

Suicide Lewisite sniffed.

He said well Purdue it's perfectly obvious that McStrangle is a good football player but don't you honestly feel that the bulk of the credit for the Radish River resurgence should be put where it belongs?

He said people are beginning to realize that I assembled this gridiron masterpiece and that under my expert guidance its climb to the heights was inevitable.

He said they're beginning to recognize the true mark of greatness that is mine.

He said I find it to be appropriate that they're forgetting lesser-lights like Stagg and Bryant and Hayes and rewarding fresh and brilliant talent with the accolades it so richly deserves.

He said the time has come for the National Football League to turn to me in order that my sparkling and innovative brand of football may revive a sport too long mired in the stagnancy of boredom.

I shrugged.

I said well Mr. Lewisite I'm certainly glad to hear you talking about something besides suicide.

Suicide Lewisite turned slowly.

He took his foot from the railing and brought it down with a thump.

He stared at me as though I was some sort of rare insect.

He said suicide Purdue?

He said do my senses deceive me or did I hear you mention suicide in connection with the name destined to become the greatest in all coaching history?

I shrugged.

I said I suppose I should be getting back to Hepzibah Dodd's place.

I said the old lady likes to chat a bit in the evening.

Suicide Lewisite said then hop to it man.

He said to the swift is the race.

He said do what thy manhood bids thee do.

I shrugged.

Suicide Lewisite said the Devil always takes the hindmost.

He said what are you waiting for?

I said well for starters you're standing on my toe.

I hobbled down to the macadam track.

I hobbled to the wrought-iron gate.

I let myself out.

I closed the gate and peeked through the bars.

On the highest point of Radish River High School stadium Suicide Lewisite stood silhouetted against the rays of the dying sun.

His legs were spread.

His hands were on his hips.

His shoulders were squared.

His head was back.

His jaw was firm.

His chest was thrown out.

Almost as though he knew I would be looking back.

...football coaches is a dime a dozen...inflation is
running wild...

Monroe D. Underwood

That evening I said Suicide Lewisite will be coaching in the
National Football League next season.

Brandy glanced up.

She said who told you that?

I said Suicide Lewisite.

Brandy said Suicide Lewisite is a little man in a big hurry.

I said well he don't seem so little when he's standing on
your toe.

Brandy said Suicide Lewisite will be extremely fortunate
if he's working on the Radish River garbage truck next season.

I said the sonofabitch must weigh two-fifty.

Brandy said the Cranberry Creek game was his first
victory in three years.

I said the trouble is he never seems to realize that he's

standing on your toe.

Brandy said Suicide Lewisite couldn't coach horses to eat hay.

I said he just stands there and stands there and stands there.

Brandy said that's enough Purdue.

I said well if he's such a bum how come he's coaching your football team?

Brandy said it's my football team in theory only.

She said and for no longer than through the coming weekend.

She said by then it'll all be over and we'll be out of here.

She said for better or hearse.

…he who hesitates ends up thirsty…

Monroe D. Underwood

I started uptown at eight in the morning.

I noticed a small tavern on a side street.

The bartender was just unlocking the door.

He said don't you think it's too early?

I shrugged.

I said hell if it's that early why are you open?

The bartender said you know I been wondering about that myself.

31

...a riot is like a visit from your mother-in-law...it
takes more to get one stopped than it does to get
it started...

Monroe D. Underwood

At two in the afternoon I continued northward.
  More or less.
  I met Sir Lennox Nilgood Fiddleduck walking south.
  He took me by the arm.
  He propped me against a tree.
  I said hi there.
  I said wass new?
  Sir Lennox said there's been a second riot.
  I said over what?
  Sir Lennox said over who started the first riot.
  He said sixty-five people have been incarcerated.
  I said oh thassawful.
  I said I thought thass sort of thing went out with the

Spanish Exposition.

Sir Lennox said sixty-five people have gone to jail Purdue.

I said my God Diddlefuck thass a hundred and thirty peoples in one swell foop.

32

...the man who's worthwhile is the man who can smile when he's holding a nail for a cross-eyed carpenter...

Monroe D. Underwood

I met Suicide Lewisite in front of the Radish River Drug Store.

He was stopping people on the sidewalk.

He was giving autographs.

He looked me up and down.

He said Purdue are you drunk?

I said well if I ain't I juss threw away six hours of my life.

Suicide Lewisite said try to be patient.

He said I'll be with you when this big autograph rush is over.

He blocked the path of a large cross-eyed woman.

He whipped out his ballpoint pen.

He said I'd be glad to.

The large cross-eyed woman said oh God Almighty!

Suicide Lewisite smiled patiently.

He said well I wouldn't go quite that far but I can readily appreciate your worshipful attitude.

The large cross-eyed woman broke into tears.

She said oh loving Jesus help me in my moment of need!

Suicide Lewisite raised his hand.

He said fret not.

He said what can I do for thee?

The large cross-eyed woman said you can get off of my toe you sonofabitch!

33

...I ain't never been drunk...merely a little less sober...

Monroe D. Underwood

It was shortly after midnight.

I sat at Brandy's kitchen table and stared into my cup of black coffee.

Brandy hovered over me like a mother eagle.

She said Sir Lennox how did you find him?

Sir Lennox looked at the floor.

He said well bloody damned drunk if you must know.

He looked at me.

He said no offense Purdue.

I shrugged.

I said fax are fax Fizzledick.

Brandy said where was he?

Sir Lennox said he was sitting on one of those chalk lines in the Radish River football stadium.

He said he was bellowing "God Save the Bloody Queen" at the top of his blooming lungs.

I said I beg your parn.

I said wass "Gol Bess America."

Sir Lennox said oh yes "God Bless America."

He said my error Purdue.

Brandy said was he alone?

Sir Lennox nodded.

I said point of order.

I said wass not alone.

I said wass with bottle Old Anchor Chain.

Sir Lennox glanced at his watch.

He looked up.

The way you look up when you hear your pilot holler banzai on the intercom.

He said blimey.

He said sixteen hours of uninterrupted drinking.

He said he must have a bloody fine physique.

Brandy leaned over my chair from the rear.

She slipped her arms around my neck.

Her breath was warm on my cheek.

There was a smile in her voice.

She said it isn't bad Sir Lennox it isn't bad.

She said Purdue what in God's name were you doing in the football stadium at that time of night?

I shrugged.

I said singing "Gol Bess America" and drinking Old Anchor Chain and watching peoples load aerial bombs in goddam scoreboard.

I said if is anybody's business.

I said which I dately grout.

Sir Lennox smiled.

He said with all those bloody aerial bombs Radish River must anticipate a complete rout of the Sycamore Center football squad.

I said well what the hell else?

I said they got a goddam five hundred goddam pound goddam gorilla playing goddam tackle.

Brandy lit a pair of cigarettes and handed one to me.

Then she doubled up laughing.

She laughed until tears came.

She dried her eyes.

She said Purdue forgive me.

She said you're just too sweet for words.

She said I've never seen you drunk before.

I shrugged.

I said well it ain't really no goddam big thing.

I said it juss got to run second to Hailey's Comet.

I was feeling much better.

I mentioned this to Brandy.

I said I'm feeling much better.

Brandy stood patting me on the shoulder.

Soothingly.

She said Sir Lennox do we have time to go uptown for a drink?

I said well by God what a hell of an idea.

Sir Lennox said yes the local pub doesn't close until two o'clock.

I said I don't know what time it closes but I know what time it opens.

I said less get rolling.

Brandy said Purdue you're going beddy-bye.

I said what am I a goddam outcast?
I said hell I ain't had leprosy in over a month.
Brandy took my hand.
She pulled me to my feet.
She said big guy you're wonderful.
She said I love you till I can hardly stand it.
She said now you're going to bed.
I shrugged.
I said when will you be back?
Brandy ran her fingers back and forth through my crew cut and her tongue back and forth along my lips.
She said baby you'll be the very first to know.

34

Consider now that bitter tale
About the missing horseshoe nail
What brought about a kingdom's fall
Which matters not to me at all
Because I never ride a horse
And this means that I walk of course
And I'm reminded when I walk
I got a hole in my left sock…

Monroe D. Underwood

I heard Brandy come in.

I felt her sit on the edge of the bed.

I lifted the pillow from my head.

I opened one eye.

Radish River Friday sunshine was blasting into the room like a rocket attack.

I looked at Brandy's tiny alarm dock.

It sounded like a pile driver.

It said ten minutes after twelve.

I put the pillow back on my head.

Brandy took it off.

She was wearing her brown robe.

There was a white ribbon in her thick dark wavy hair.

She smiled her wonderfully warm smile.

In her soft husky-sweet voice she said good-morning.

She said almost.

I said you're beautiful.

I said go away.

Brandy said Purdue I'll never go away.

She said not for very long.

I said that's how it seems to be working out.

Brandy said how do you feel?

I shrugged.

I said if I told you how I feel I'd spoil your day.

I said I thought you were going to wake me up when you came in last night.

Brandy said last night you would have slept through the Battle of Midway.

I said ah ha!

I said that explains it.

I said I swallowed an aircraft carrier.

Brandy said besides I didn't get in until nearly dawn.

I said you and Sir Lennox must have been doing some serious drinking.

Brandy said no I got rid of Sir Lennox in a hurry.

She said he travels the fastest who travels alone.

She said Kipling.

I said Tinker to Evers to Chance.

I said Adams.

Brandy said John or John Quincy?

I shrugged.

Brandy said get up and come into the kitchen for coffee.

She said I want to talk to you about the situation in Radish River.

She said this little town is coming to a boil.

She said by kickoff time tomorrow night the lid may blow off.

I said Radish River never had a lid.

I said we should go home and let Doctor Ho Ho Ho have it.

Brandy said Purdue Radish River is like the horseshoe nail.

She said if we lose it the kingdom goes down the drain.

I said yeah how did that go?

Brandy said no matter.

I said for want of a nail the shoe was lost.

Brandy said yes.

She said Purdue we aren't whipped yet.

I said for want of a shoe the horse was lost.

Brandy said I'm going to play a long shot.

I said this wasn't a racehorse Brandy.

I said it was a horse that carried a rider to battle.

Brandy said perhaps we can still turn the tables on Ho Ho Ho.

I said they lost the battle on account of this rider didn't show up.

I said he couldn't get there without his horse you see.

Brandy nodded.

She said Purdue you'll never learn will you?

She reached for the belt of her robe.

I sat up.

I said look Brandy why don't we go into the kitchen and have coffee?

I said I'm anxious to hear about the situation in Radish River.

35

...1919 was a bad year...President Wilson had a stroke and there was a big flu epidemic and they had a hurricane in Florida and a tornado in Minnesota and a volcano blowed up in Java and Zapata got ambushed in Mexico and the Sox throwed the Series to Cincinnati and the 18th Amendment got passed and my mother-in-law showed up for Thanksgiving dinner...

Monroe D. Underwood

Brandy poured my third cup of scalding black coffee.

She said Purdue will you believe me when I tell you that Doctor Ho Ho Ho is reportedly two hundred years old?

I shrugged.

I said I didn't know that they've been making yogurt that long.

Brandy said where Doctor Ho Ho Ho is there has always been big trouble.

She said he doesn't care who wins just so long as there's enough misery to go around.

She said among global leaders Ho Ho Ho is referred to as The Fifth Horseman.

I shrugged.

I said maybe he's the guy who lost that horseshoe nail.

Brandy said Ho Ho Ho's list of catastrophic credits is downright mind-bending.

She said he started the Boxer War in 1900 and the Russo-Japanese conflict in 1904.

She said he arranged for an iceberg to foul the route of the *Titanic* in 1912 and he was responsible for the assassination of Archduke Ferdinand in 1914.

She said it was Ho Ho Ho who really sank the *Lusitania* in 1915.

She said it was Ho Ho Ho who persuaded Germany to invade Russia and Japan to attack Pearl Harbor in 1941.

She said four wars between Israel and the Arab nations have been attributed to Ho Ho Ho and the Cuban missile crisis was a direct result of his manipulations.

She said throw in a few thousand fires and floods and explosions and epidemics and you'll have a small fraction of Doctor Ho Ho Ho's deadly enterprises.

I shrugged.

I said I got a hunch that the sonofabitch has been messing around with the Chicago White Sox.

Brandy smiled.

She said no Purdue.

She said not since 1919.

36

…the big difference between radios and television
sets is all the radios should get dumped in the
Atlantic Ocean and the television sets should get
dumped in the Pacific…

Monroe D. Underwood

I finished my coffee and stood up.

I said so what's on the docket for this afternoon?

Brandy said you just mosey up to town and nose
around.

I said where will you be?

Brandy said Purdue I'm going to make a move.

She said we've sat on our hands long enough.

She said I'm going to put Hepzibah Dodd away for
a time.

She said I'm going to become the old gal's granddaughter who has dropped in from out of town.

She said the Radish River Radio and Television Shop

has a For Sale sign in its window.

She said I'm going to buy it and try to parlay it into the grand finale of Doctor Ho Ho Ho's career.

37

...the Royal Bengal Lancers got disbanded just as soon as they got done lancing all them Royal Bengals...

Monroe D. Underwood

I went into the little tavern at the south end of Radish River.
Both of its big plate-glass windows had been broken.
The bartender looked up.
He said oh my God.
He said you again.
He said ain't you made it home yet?
I shrugged.
I said I must have.
I said I'm wearing different colored socks.
He said I just noticed that.
He said one's black.
He said the other one's sort of pink.
He said with hair yet.

I shrugged.

I said look pal nobody's perfect.

He said I got to admit you made a very big impression in here yesterday morning.

I said doing what?

He said reciting "Barbara Fritchie" and singing "America the Beautiful."

He said also conducting two hours of close-order drill.

I said for who?

He said well let's see now.

He said there was me and Lefty Bates and Ebenezer Roberts and the beer truck driver and two nuns from St. Rockne's Church.

I said I didn't know that nuns hung out in taverns.

He said they don't.

He said they just happened to be passing by.

I shrugged.

I said how did it go?

He said oh it went just great until you marched the whole damn platoon out through that right-hand plate-glass window.

I said well that don't explain what happened to the left-hand window.

He said that got busted when you marched us back in.

I said I see.

I said thanks for not getting me locked up.

He said oh I would of got you locked up in a hurry only I couldn't locate the chief of police.

He said what the hell do you do for a living?

He said besides conducting close-order drills.

I said I'm a writer for a sports rag.

He said what's its name?

I said *Sports Rag*.

He said oh yeah *Sports Rag*.

He said I got a subscription.

I said what's happening in town?

He said well the mayor just issued a proclamation.

He said he's granting amnesty to everybody in the Radish River jail effective eight o'clock tomorrow morning.

He said if there's any more trouble he'll get the governor to mobilize the 000th Field Artillery.

I said the hooth?

He said the 000th Field Artillery is our local National Guard unit.

He said it ain't exactly the Royal Bengal Lancers but it's all we got.

I said where was it during the war?

He said well fifty percent of it was AWOL.

He said fifty-five percent of it was on a sick call.

I said where did that extra five percent come from?

He said probably the replacement depot.

...the trouble with tight slacks is the women
what can't wear 'em does and the women what
can don't...

Monroe D. Underwood

About four in the afternoon a beautifully assembled young
lady strolled into the tavern.

She wore smoked glasses with saucer-sized lenses.

Her bosom strained impatiently against the glistening
satin of her baby-blue blouse.

Her navy-blue knit slacks looked like they'd been applied
with an airbrush.

She sat at the far end of the bar.

The bartender nearly bowed a tendon getting to her.

They talked for a couple of minutes.

He poured her a shot of bourbon with a short glass of
water on the side.

She drank it without making a face.

She barely touched her water.

She smiled at me.

I smiled back.

I bought her a drink.

She drank it.

She bought me a drink.

I drank it.

I bought her a drink.

She stuck the tip of her tongue out at me.

It was very pink.

She wiggled it.

I fell off my barstool.

She went out.

The bartender helped me up.

I said who the hell was that?

He said that's the granddaughter of the old broad who owns the football team.

He said her name is Ophelia Dodd.

He said she told me that she just bought the Radish River Radio and Television Shop.

He said she told me that she'll be entering a chariot in the Annual Radish River Roman Chariot Race.

39

...what where and when ain't never nowhere near
as important as how...

Monroe D. Underwood

It had begun to rain.

It slashed at the windows of the old house and it
rumbled on the roof.

Brandy winked at me.

She said oh Purdue you dissolute old rake you.

She said I've completely underestimated you.

I said hey I knew it was you all the time.

Brandy said how?

I said your slacks were so tight I recognized the mole
on your hip.

Brandy said it isn't a mole.

She said it's a birthmark.

I shrugged.

I said well whatever.

Brandy said it isn't on my hip.

She said it's on my thigh.

I shrugged.

I said well wherever.

Brandy said Purdue I think you'd better get reacquainted with the terrain.

She stood and began to unbutton her baby-blue satin blouse.

She said now.

I shrugged.

I said well whenever.

40

...any situation what demands the grace of God is
already beyond the grace of God...

Monroe D. Underwood

The silence in the darkness of Brandy's bedroom was long and lilac-scented.

I broke it by saying I have a suggestion.

Brandy said Purdue I'm always open to suggestions.

I said that wasn't what I was going to suggest.

I said I was going to suggest that we get some sleep.

I said you see there is so very little to be gained by doing anything else.

I said we've already busted every record in the book.

I said again.

Brandy sat up.

She lit a pair of cigarettes for us.

She placed our ice-cold glass ashtray in its long-appointed location.

Right on my navel.

She said I hate to give up so early.

She said this may be our last night in Radish River.

She said the manure is about to hit the fan.

She said when it does I want you to meet me at the Radish River Drug Store as soon as possible.

I shrugged.

I said without packing?

Brandy said our suitcases will be in the car.

I said you're calling the shots.

Brandy said Purdue if I'm ever going to be right this had damned well better be the time.

She said it's possible that I'm verging on a blunder of astronomical proportions.

I said by the way what the hell could you possibly want with a radio and television business?

Brandy said I'll never open the doors.

She said the Radish River Radio and Television Shop has a chariot that's eligible for the big race.

She said that chariot was all I really wanted.

I said who's going to drive the damn thing?

Brandy said I am.

She said by the grace of God that is.

I shrugged.

I said now all you need is a horse.

Brandy said I have one.

She said a seventeen-year-old veteran by the name of Lochinvar X.

She said the old darling used to run at Sportsman's Park and he won his share.

I said wouldn't a trotter or a pacer be better-suited to

a chariot?

Brandy said not to a Roman chariot.

She said and most certainly not to my purposes.

I said do you know the first damn thing about horses?

Brandy said Purdue I was born in Nebraska.

She said as a kid I finished second in the National Bareback Finals at Omaha.

I said Brandy I don't really believe you ever finished second at anything.

Brandy said well I might have won it but my mare was in season.

She said so was I.

I shrugged.

I said you still are.

Brandy killed our cigarettes.

She lifted the ashtray from my navel.

She said Purdue your perceptivity is little short of breathtaking.

41

...peace ain't nothing but a breathing-spell between wars...

Monroe D. Underwood

Saturday dawned a crisp cloudless blue.

At eight o'clock Mayor Bradford Boone swung open the doors of the Radish River jail.

Seventy-seven people spilled into freedom.

There were sixty-five rioters and a pair of kidnappers and three burglars and four rapists and a murderer and a shoplifter and one very pissed-off Radish River chief of police who had been mysteriously missing since Wednesday.

In the interests of peace the governor of the State of Illinois had mobilized the 000th Field Artillery.

Twenty minutes following assembly of the 000th Field Artillery there was a riot.

Among members of the 000th Field Artillery.

42

On the seventh day God was just resting
And for Him that was something right new
He'd worked like the Devil for six days
And He'd sure had aplenty to do
But then as He took it real easy
He was seized in the grip of remorse
'Cause He still hadn't done nothing perfect
So He spent that day making the horse…

Monroe D. Underwood

By seven that evening the Radish River High School stadium
was brimming with wild-eyed locals waving banners that
would have appalled the goddess Kali.

Five chariots were admitted to the grounds at seven-
thirty.

Four represented Radish River businesses and the
managements had gone all out to stress those services
offered to the community.

The fifth chariot had been entered by the Radish River Police Department.

The Radish River High School band blew a long fanfare and the chariots passed on parade around the track.

In addition to its driver the Radish River Bakery's chariot carried a bikini-clad young damsel who would toss doughnuts to the crowd during the great race.

The Radish River Plumbing Company's chariot was a bathtub mounted on bicycle wheels.

The Radish River Funeral Home's entry was a beautiful thing appropriately draped in black velvet and dark purple crepe and studded with any number of lilies.

On its left side was a small neatly lettered sign that read WHY NOT GO FIRST CLASS?

On its right side was another reading DIE NOW PAY LATER E-Z FINANCING AVAILABLE.

Its driver was a bent and white-bearded old man who carried a large hourglass and a scythe.

The Radish River Police Department's vehicle was equipped with flashing lights and a siren.

It was driven by the Radish River chief of police and accompanied by the entire police force.

It carried a single sign which said CRIME DOESN'T PAY BUT IT PAYS A LOT BETTER THAN BEING A COP YOU CHEAP BASTARDS YOU.

As their chariot rolled in review the Radish River policemen circulated through the crowd and passed their hats.

Their harvest was not particularly bountiful.

It amounted to one dollar and eighty-nine cents and half of a sauerkraut sandwich and a photograph of a fat woman trying to take her girdle off although there were many who insisted that it was a photograph of a fat woman trying to put her girdle on.

During these activities somebody broke into the Radish River Bank and made off with thirty-six thousand dollars and a nearly full March of Dimes card.

The Radish River Radio and Television Shop chariot was painted gold and rigged with speakers and during the parade lap it played the Heidelberg Grenadiers Polka Mazurka and Military Band's recording of *Alte Kameraden* at something like fifty million decibels more than the human ear can tolerate.

The chariots pulled to a stop on the track beyond the north end zone.

Brandy said it was supposed to play "Over the Waves" but I thought you'd appreciate *Alte Kameraden*.

I said I like your Roman toga.

Brandy said guess what's under it.

I said just you.

Brandy said just me.

I shrugged.

Brandy said Purdue meet Lochinvar X.

Lochinvar X. was a huge bald-faced blue roan with three white stockings.

His back was swayed and his knees were knobby and his shins bore the scars of the long racetrack years but there was still fire in the old fellow's eyes.

I said where did you round him up?

Brandy said I rented him from a farm family just a few miles out of town.

She said I left my Porsche as a deposit.

She said they've been using him as a plow horse.

I said a Thoroughbred pulling a plow?

Brandy said it was love at first sight.

She said if we get out of this mess alive I'm going to buy him and put him up in a decent home outside Chicago.

She said fields of clover and a cold clear stream.

She said a place where he can dream and hear a friendly word.

She said Lochinvar X. will have that much from life so help me God.

She blinked away a tear.

Lochinvar X. gave Brandy a great slurping kiss.

I brushed at my eyes with the back of my hand.

I said damned dust.

Brandy said yes isn't it terrible?

She said with no wind and after all that rain.

43

...witch doctors ain't doing so well these days...
there just ain't enough sick witches to go around...
Monroe D. Underwood

In the locker room the trainer of the Radish River Possumcats
said hey Coach where's the medical alcohol?

He said I think Blunderfoot got a infection.

Suicide Lewisite said well if Blunderfoot got a infection
it just got to be where Blunderfoot sits down on account of
that is where Blunderfoot takes most of his wear and tear.

He said there's a jug of medical alcohol in my office.

The trainer said the jug is there but the alcohol ain't.

He said it must of evaporated.

Suicide Lewisite said yeah well that's your department.

He said right now I got to introduce our new chaplain.

The new chaplain's name was Witch Doctor Mulugu
Ugununu.

Witch Doctor Mulugu Ugununu stood eight feet tall in

his bare feet.

He wore a zebra skin and there was a bone through his nose.

He got right down to business by shuffling around and waving his arms and making little grunting sounds.

Suicide Lewisite watched with obvious admiration.

He said have you ever met a witch doctor before?

I said no but I know a couple dentists I'm not so sure of.

Suicide Lewisite said well this Mulugu Ugununu is a real good one and I understand he's a lead-pipe cinch to make the Witch Doctor Hall of Fame.

Witch Doctor Mulugu Ugununu had warmed to his work.

The tempo had been stepped up and his shuffle had been replaced by kicks not unlike those common to the Charleston.

Suicide Lewisite said ah ha!

He said Mulugu Ugununu is preparing to put a curse on the Sycamore Center Ridgelings.

The dance went on and Mulugu Ugununu had begun to move in a large circle with his hands high over his head.

It was obvious that something big was in the offing.

Suicide Lewisite laughed delightedly.

He clapped his hands and stamped a foot in rhythm.

As the witch doctor passed in front of us Suicide Lewisite yelled sock it to 'em Ugununu!

Witch Doctor Mulugu Ugununu let out a bloodcurdling shriek.

He bounded a yard into the air.

When he came down he began to pop rapidly around on one foot.

He cuddled his other foot tenderly to his groin.

He bellowed several things in his native tongue and two or three in mine.

All unprintable.

His eyes were wide open.

His eyeballs rolled loosely.

His teeth were bared.

Slippery Sleighballs said well I don't know what he's doing to the Sycamore Center Ridgelings but he is sure scaring the hell out of me.

Suicide Lewisite was pale.

He said Holy Christ.

He said maybe I better stop him before he slaps a curse on the whole goddam country.

I shrugged.

I said I noticed that things began to pick up right after you stepped on his toe.

44

...when Darwin said man descended from apes
the major complaints come from William Jennings
Bryan and the apes...

Monroe D. Underwood

In the pregame huddle Suicide Lewisite implored his players
to give their all for Radish River.

Zanzibar McStrangle burped.

The Sycamore Center Ridgelings fanned onto the field.

The Radish River Possumcats went out to a roar that
could have been heard in Yokohama.

Zanzibar McStrangle lurched toward the football.

His kickoff landed on the roof of the Radish River
Drug Store.

The game was under way.

The referee placed a new ball on the Sycamore Center
twenty yard line.

Zanzibar McStrangle picked it up.

He peeled it and ate it.

Radish River was penalized fifty yards.

It was explained that fifty yards was the standard penalty for peeling and eating footballs.

With the ball on the Radish River thirty yard line Sycamore Center went into punt formation.

Zanzibar McStrangle grabbed the punter and heaved him into the hotdog stand thereby busting a gallon jar of mustard.

Radish River was penalized twenty yards.

Fifteen yards for unnecessary roughness and five yards because mustard is very expensive.

Suicide Lewisite said I wonder if the Radish River Drug Store sells arsenic in the large economy size.

I said I rather imagine you'd need a prescription.

With the ball on our ten yard line Sycamore Center again prepared to punt.

The punter saw Zanzibar McStrangle coming.

He threw the ball into the air and ran for his life.

Zanzibar McStrangle caught the ball and he was in the clear when somebody threw a banana onto the field.

Zanzibar McStrangle stopped cold.

He discarded the ball in favor of the banana.

In the ensuing confusion a Sycamore Center player picked up the ball and ran for a touchdown.

Suicide Lewisite stared at me.

He said that medical alcohol didn't evaporate.

He said once a monkey always a monkey.

He said by the way have you heard of any new ways of committing suicide?

Zanzibar McStrangle had an amazing first half.

He took no chances.

He tackled everybody.

With or without the ball.

On either team.

With one herculean effort he tackled both teams and the entire Radish River High School band.

With another he tackled the officials and seven ushers and four hundred spectators.

With time in the half running out we were trailing 6-0 and we had lost more than two thousand yards in penalties.

Suddenly Suicide Lewisite made a wild dash for the timekeeper.

He grabbed the astonished official's pistol.

He tried to shoot himself.

When the blank cartridge went off both teams headed for the lockers.

Suicide Lewisite went into the maintenance shed where he attempted to tie a hangman's noose in a tow chain.

I stayed behind to watch the big Roman chariot race.

45

...I don't know what *aloha oe* means in Honolulu
but I can sure tell you what *jigjig* means in Suva...

Monroe D. Underwood

The race was to consist of ten laps.

Brandy and Lochinvar X. had drawn the outside position.

The chariots broke cleanly enough.

Brandy checked Lochinvar X. and took him to the rail.

They went around closely bunched with the funeral parlor driver brandishing his scythe and the scantily attired young thing on the bakery chariot flinging doughnuts in a great many directions.

As they lit into the second lap the police force chariot opened up a two-length lead.

In the far turn the plumbing company chariot made a run at the front-runner.

Its valiant effort to pass on the inside resulted in an utterly horrendous collision that demolished both chariots.

The plumbing company driver made a breathtaking leap from his doomed vehicle in time to save his life and receive a reckless driving ticket from the Radish River chief of police.

Midway through the third lap the girl on the bakery chariot uncorked a wild doughnut which struck the funeral home driver squarely between the eyes and rendered the unfortunate fellow instantly senseless.

The funeral home chariot smashed into a wall and capsized.

In the pileup the scythe was busted and most of the lilies were ruined.

Now the race had boiled down to the bakery chariot and Brandy.

They swept along hub-to-hub with the big crowd whooping it up and the Radish River High School band just blowing the socks off of "El Capitan."

Out of the corner of my eye I saw the scoreboard lights flicker briefly.

I glanced in that direction.

I stood transfixed.

From the door of the gigantic scoreboard filed a great many men wearing bright red uniforms and white helmets and carrying sleek automatic rifles.

My blood ran cold.

Doctor Ho Ho Ho's troops were in Radish River.

I stumbled to the edge of the track.

I gestured to Brandy.

I pointed to the scoreboard.

Brandy nodded and smiled grimly.

She looked back and winked as her chariot plunged into the turn.

When the Radish River Bakery entry came by again Brandy was several lengths back.

At some point in the backstretch she had left her chariot and now she sat firmly astride Lochinvar X.

The giant blue roan came hammering down the stretch. His ears were laid back.

His white stockings flashed scissors-like as he devoured distance with Triple Crown strides.

Reflections of the Radish River stadium floodlights flared in his eyes.

Lochinvar X. was running his last race and he was giving it all he had.

Brandy Alexander was crouched low over the neck of the ancient warrior.

She was stroking him and speaking into his ear.

Her toga was up around her neck.

There was nothing under it but Brandy Alexander.

As Lochinvar X. thundered by I saw Brandy reach back to jerk at a strand of leather.

Suddenly Lochinvar X. was free of the chariot.

The old campaigner's head went up.

He clattered around the bend and made for the backstretch.

The driverless gold chariot came barreling in his wake.

As far as the turn.

At that point it continued straight ahead.

It jumped a curb.

It bounded across twenty yards of grass.

With an awe-inspiring crash it plowed headlong into the front of the magnificent Radish River scoreboard.

The chariot flipped over.

Its wheels wobbled to a stop.

At that moment it lit up like a fluorescent bulb.

It buckled and curled and dissolved in a torrent of vivid blue electrical flame.

The scoreboard rocked and rumbled.

It hissed ominously.

Then tons and tons of aerial bombs began to go off.

There were small explosions and large explosions and middle-sized explosions.

There was general hell to pay.

It was a cross between the Battle of the Bulge and the end of the world.

That is just a guess of course.

I missed the former and I have no intentions of attending the latter.

From horizon to horizon the sky was an unholy orange hue.

The ground shuddered violently beneath my feet.

The decrepit Radish River High School building emitted a prolonged groan and caved in.

The flagpole swayed wildly from side to side and Old Glory snapped and crackled high above the unbelievable scene.

The Radish River High School band played "The Star-Spangled Banner."

I shook my head.

Fort McHenry had never seen the likes of this.

The Radish River fans stood to applaud the halftime show.

The Radish River High School band played "America the Beautiful."

The great scoreboard began to lift slowly into the air.

At an altitude of approximately fifteen feet it paused.

It hovered there surrounded by swirling smoke.

Then in a blinding deafening blast it vanished completely.

The Radish River fans cheered vociferously.

The Radish River High School band played "The Stars and Stripes Forever."

Where the scoreboard had stood I saw a huge hole in the stadium floor.

Into this hole staggered a great many men wearing tattered bright red uniforms and battered white helmets.

There wasn't a single sleek automatic rifle in sight.

Doctor Ho Ho Ho's troops were leaving Radish River.

The Radish River High School band played "Aloha Oe."

I looked for Brandy and saw the broad rump of Lochinvar X. go through the gate and into the tormented night.

The lights went out.

I shrugged.

I headed for the Radish River Drug Store.

46

...if all the rabbits ever gets together we gonna
have a lot more rabbits than we already got...
                                    Monroe D. Underwood

It was after eleven o'clock.

I sat on the steps of the Radish River Drug Store.

I smoked a V-shaped Camel and watched anxiously for
Brandy's car.

Radish River had busted at the seams and all the stuffing
was coming out.

Half of the business district windows had been
shattered.

Drunks sprawled in doorways and gutters.

I heard the drum of feet pounding up and down the
night alleys.

Now and then a man would shout or a woman would
scream.

I watched an angry rabbit pursue two terrified Great

Danes down the middle of the street.

From around the corner came the sound of singing.

"We'll Be Standing 'Neath the Streetlight at Ten on Friday Night Singing Songs of Love in Harmony."

Probably the boys of the 000th Field Artillery.

They had an excellent tenor.

Mayor Bradford Boone came by.

He was leading a large group of men.

He carried a rope with a nasty-looking loop at one end.

Three of the men carried spades and one had an enormous white leather Bible with gilt-edged pages and a gold cross on its front.

Mayor Bradford Boone said Purdue have you seen Suicide Lewisite?

I shrugged.

I said not since the end of the first half.

The bartender from the little tavern came running up.

He was carrying a pick.

He said hey I just heard that Lewisite is trying to shoot himself with the West Side American Legion cannon.

There was a loud report from the west.

There was an odd fluttering sound overhead.

There was an explosion.

The Radish River City Hall went up in a vast cloud of flying debris.

Mayor Boone said let's go boys.

The man with the Bible said maybe he's already dead.

Mayor Boone said that's okay.

He said we'll hang the sonofabitch anyway.

They hurried off into the darkness.

An old man limped up to me.

He shoved a topless cigar box in my direction.

He said sir would you care to contribute to the fund for a new Radish River scoreboard?

I threw a dollar into the box.

The old man went away.

I shrugged.

In Radish River they take their football very seriously.

47

…When you gets to checking contents of the
local loony bin
You'll find we got more loonies out than we got
loonies in…

Monroe D. Underwood

The silver-gray Porsche arrived just short of midnight and I got in.

I said Brandy where the hell have you been?

I said a man could get killed in this goddam insane asylum.

Brandy said sorry Purdue.

She said I rode Lochinvar X. back to the farm.

She said I bought him and made arrangements to have him shipped to Chicago.

She said I was nearly here when I had to stop for Suicide Lewisite.

I said I thought he committed suicide with the American

Legion cannon.

Brandy said he missed.

She said the poor man was frightened out of his wits.

I said well he should have been.

I said he leveled the Radish River City Hall and there was a lynch mob on his trail.

Brandy said that wasn't it.

She said he had just stepped on Zanzibar McStrangle's toe.

She said I took him down the back streets to the Radish River freight yard and he caught an outbound boxcar.

She said it was full of footballs.

48

...firstest time I ever seen one I didn't even know
how it worked...

Monroe D. Underwood

Seventy-five miles north of Radish River Brandy pulled into
the parking lot of a little motel.

She said Purdue run into the office and get us a room.

I shrugged.

I said why don't we just drive straight through?

I said hell I'm not tired.

Brandy said it isn't a matter of being tired.

She said I can't drive to Chicago wearing this damned
Roman toga.

She said there's nothing under it but me.

She turned up the dash lights.

She said look.

I looked.

I said oh yeah.

I said that.

I said I've already seen it.

I said so have fifteen thousand people in Radish River stadium.

Brandy said well what the hell Purdue.

She said if they'd never seen one they didn't know what it was.

49

…you show me a man with a ashtray on his
navel and I'll show you a man with a warm belly
button…

Monroe D. Underwood

The room was dark and our cigarettes glowed ruby-red and
our ashtray was on my navel.

I said Brandy don't you ever get tired of dark rooms with
our cigarettes glowing ruby-red and our ashtray on my navel?

Brandy said never.

I said well I do.

Brandy said Purdue do you want to do it another way?

I said don't be silly.

I said there ain't no other ways left.

Brandy said sex isn't the subject of discussion.

She said what would you change about this situation?

I shrugged.

I said I'd put the ashtray on *your* navel.

50

…oncet I knowed a feller what got a short-circuit in his hearing aid…improved his hearing but his wife went deaf…

Monroe D. Underwood

Brandy said well thank God it's over.

She said it'll be put down as a stupid accident and there'll be no federal investigation.

I said that was probably the shortest military invasion in history.

Brandy said Purdue we got lucky.

She said it was a beautifully planned assault.

She said if it hadn't been for you Ho Ho Ho would have brought it off without a hitch.

I shrugged.

I said hell I didn't do anything but stumble around town.

Brandy said on the night you got drunk you mentioned that they were loading aerial bombs into the scoreboard at midnight.

She said that was the kicker.

She said I sent you to bed and then I got rid of Sir Lennox Nilgood Fiddleduck.

She said after that I did some serious snooping.

She said Purdue the scoreboard contained considerably more than aerial bombs.

She said there were thousands of hand grenades and millions of rounds of automatic rifle ammunition.

She said it was jammed to the rafters.

She said Doctor Ho Ho Ho's advance party had surreptitiously gained control of the scoreboard and converted it into a combination ammunition dump and point of entry.

She said the first elements of his invasion force were to march onto the football field and the Radish River fans would have assumed them to be a crack drill team imported for the halftime show.

She said virtually the entire Radish River populace was in the stadium and Ho Ho Ho planned to annihilate it.

I shrugged.

I said well you can't win 'em all.

I said he just picked the wrong damn town.

Brandy said Radish River was the perfect choice.

She said it's remote and its people were caught up in a football frenzy and it had that monstrous scoreboard.

She said everything was made to order.

I said I'll bet old Ho Ho Ho thought he'd been ambushed by the whole goddam United States Army.

Brandy said Ho Ho Ho knew what was happening but his troops didn't.

She said they panicked.

I said how did you manage to blow the scoreboard?

Brandy said I brought a team of specialists from Langley.

She said they worked on the chariot for twenty-four hours.

She said when they were finished that vehicle weighed nearly half a ton and it was an electrical catastrophe on wheels.

She said once the race was under way I threw a switch that set up a massive short circuit keyed to occur the instant the chariot wheels stopped turning.

I said well what if you'd had to pull up for some reason?

Brandy pressed my hand.

She said then we wouldn't be in this dark room with our cigarettes glowing ruby-red and our ashtray on your navel.

She took the ashtray from my navel.

She placed it on her own navel.

She said Purdue is that better?

51

...the only differences between a tenor and a bass
is a soprano and a baritone...

Monroe D. Underwood

Illinois dawn poked slim gray fingers into our motel room.

I stretched and yawned.

I said well I suppose Doctor Ho Ho Ho is halfway to
Manchuria and Sir Lennox Nilgood Fiddleduck is en route
to London.

Brandy said no he's in the Radish River jail.

I said who?

I said which one?

Brandy said both.

She said Purdue they're the same man.

I blinked.

I said Ho Ho Ho and Fiddleduck?

Brandy said oh yes.

She said Fiddleduck came to me with oodles of

identification.

She said I bought his story but I began to become suspicious when he kept insisting that Doctor Ho Ho Ho just had to be Chinese and that he would pop up in Gunther's Woods.

She said ten special operatives nailed Fiddleduck shortly after the scoreboard blew up.

She said he was singing tenor with the 000th Field Artillery.

I said yeah I heard them.

I said "We'll Be Standing 'Neath the Streetlight at Ten on Friday Night Singing Songs of Love in Harmony."

Brandy said gee I like those words.

She said what's the name of the song?

I shrugged.

I said I thought Ho Ho Ho sang bass.

I said is that all you had to go on?

Brandy said certainly not.

She said on Thursday night I learned that Fiddleduck wears leopard-skin shorts.

A scowl crept into my voice.

I said how the hell did you do that?

A smile crept into Brandy's voice.

She said why?

I said because goddammit I want to know goddammit that's why goddammit!

Brandy said Purdue don't be naive.

I said well I'll be a dirty no-good rotten miserable low-down double-jointed web-toed flap-lipped sand-bagging triple-fractured three-eyed bastard son of a nine-legged flaming dipped-in-owl-manure goddam giraffe!

I said from New Caledonia.

I said how was he?

Brandy said well let's see.

She tried to stop laughing.

She couldn't.

She said he was above average.

She said for a two-hundred-year-old man that is.

I didn't say anything.

Brandy took the ashtray from her navel.

She rolled onto me.

She hadn't been laughing after all.

Her tears dropped to my face.

They were very salty.

She said Purdue you're jealous.

She said praise God you're jealous!

I shrugged.

Brandy said don't be jealous.

She said it was all in the line of duty.

She said I had to fix him so he couldn't trail me to the scoreboard.

I said well that explains why the sonofabitch was singing tenor.

I said you screwed the bass out of him.

Brandy put her face close to mine.

She said strictly business.

She ran her fingers through my crew cut.

She said there's a tremendous difference between business and pleasure.

She said Purdue I am about to show you the tremendous difference.

Brandy showed me the tremendous difference.

The difference was tremendous.

52

...cats is strange creatures...they is real quiet all day...then they make love at three in the morning and wake up half the county...

Monroe D. Underwood

Wallace peered at me with sleepy eyes.

He said don't you think it's too early?

I shrugged.

I said hell if it's that early why are you open?

Wallace said you know I been wondering about that myself.

I sat at the bar.

I shook my head.

Wallace said what's the matter?

I said nothing important.

I said I just got the feeling that I've lived this moment before.

Wallace said yeah that happens to me every so often.

He said last time was when Old Dad Underwood and Shorty Connors come in here and got to talking about guitars.

The door opened.

Old Dad Underwood and Shorty Connors came in.

They sat at the bar.

They got to talking about guitars.

Shorty Connors said I got a big problem making a F chord.

Old Dad Underwood said me too.

He said oncet I asked a guy how to make a good F chord.

He said this guy tole me I should just mash a handful of strings and hit 'er a lick.

Shorty Connors said how did it work out?

Old Dad Underwood said not too good.

He said we still can't get the cat from under the couch.

Shorty Connors said last year I wrote to Segovia and asked him how to make a good F chord.

He said Segovia never answered.

He said neither did Chet Atkins.

He said now I don't feel so bad.

Old Dad Underwood said a guitar is just like a woman's body.

Shorty Connors said yeah I see lots like that at the shopping center.

Old Dad Underwood said I don't mean the shape.

Shorty Connors said well I got a sister-in-law what is completely unstrung.

Old Dad Underwood said I am talking about the way a woman's body responds to your caresses.

Shorty Connors said well here we are back on F chords.

Wallace said I just got the feeling that I have lived this

moment before I lived this moment before.

He stared at me.

He said Chance you look pale.

He said what kind of feeling did you just get?

I said I just got the feeling that I left my suitcase in Brandy Alexander's automobile.

53

...Jimmy the Greek is a genius...he can tell you exackly why a team is going to win by seven points and when the game is over he can tell you exackly why it lost by twenty-one...

Monroe D. Underwood

Wallace said I was reading in the morning paper about that Radish River town.

He said seems they had a little trouble down there last night.

I said Wallace the mind boggles.

Wallace said some gorilla derailed a freight train.

He said the paper had an article on one of their football players.

I said Zanzibar McStrangle?

Wallace said yeah out of Barnum-Bailey.

I said what about him?

Wallace said he's going to be in the Super Bowl next year.

I said doing what?

I said eating footballs?

Wallace said he's going to play the whole damn National Football League.

I shrugged.

I said what's the spread?

Wallace said if you go with McStrangle you got to give thirteen points.

54

...the world's most welcome words, I think,
Are simply these..."Lets have a drink."...

Monroe D. Underwood

Betsy came in about midnight.

She motioned to Wallace.

Wallace blushed.

He came over to us.

Betsy said thanks for the call.

She said I thought you should know that your diagnosis was amazingly accurate.

She said he's drunk.

Wallace said well he's been working on it since eight this morning.

I said less us all stann an sing "Gol Bess America."

I said later I will favor this assemblage with a recital of "Farber Bitchy."

Wallace said well at least there ain't been no close-order

drill yet.

Betsy said cool it Wallace.

I said wut thoo free hore!

Wallace said sorry Betsy.

I said rye the blight mank farsh!

Betsy said me too.

I said hattery balt!

Wallace said oh merciful Christ.

I said halt you bassers!

Betsy said ain't it the truth?

I said you sumbisshes bare halt!

Betsy said Chance I'm going to take you home.

I said fum sucking army.

Betsy said come on honey let's go.

I said I can't go.

I said I gonno goddam suitcase.

Betsy said your suitcase is at home.

She said a sweet little old lady delivered it an hour ago.

She said it seems you left it at the bus station.

I said thass was nice of her.

Betsy said yes wasn't it?

She said I simply can't imagine how she got our address because there's never been a tag on your suitcase.

I said battery attenchut!

Betsy said she was such an interesting old lady and I believe she said her name was Dodd.

I said forward harch!

Betsy said she was very old but she wore lilac perfume and Autumn Rose lipstick.

I said in cadence count!

Betsy said I watched her leave and she was driving a

silver-gray Porsche.

I said hut two three four!

Betsy said hardly the vehicle for a woman so old.

Betsy said just as she was getting into her car a big man came by and snatched her purse.

I groaned.

I said oh that poor bastard.

Betsy said what was that?

I said why that dirty bastard.

Betsy said the old lady caught him in three strides.

She said she punched him out.

Betsy whistled.

She said what footwork.

Betsy said what a right uppercut.

She said absolutely remarkable for a woman of her years.

I said hut two three four!

Betsy peered at me.

She said Chance suddenly your diction seems greatly improved.

I said thut foo hee trore!

I said ass in preview!

Betsy said Chance stop it.

I said time for juss one more lil ole drink here.

Betsy gave me a pat on the cheek.

She said huh-uh sweetheart.

She said you aren't going to wiggle off the hook this time.

She said we're going to discuss that sweet little old lady in the morning.

She said at great length.

I didn't say anything.

Betsy helped me to my feet.
She pushed me toward the door.
She said forward harch!
She said hut two three four!

Of all the great wonders God gave us to see
The greatest by far you will surely agree
Is the mystical magical alibi tree...
Its succulent fruit tumbles sweet to the tooth
A tonic for age and a blessing for youth
It renders the eater immune to the truth...
And rogue becomes saint as by Holy Decree
And wrong becomes right with God's firm guarantee
In the shade of the wonderful alibi tree...
Here in hypocrisy man may abide
Here he self-justifies...here he may hide
From the sins he has sinned and the lies he has lied...
Oh Lord take the lion the lamb and the flea
Level the mountain and dry up the sea
But spare if You will Lord the alibi tree...

Monroe D. Underwood

THE CHANCE PURDUE SERIES

THE DADA CAPER

Chance Purdue may be better at a lot of things than he is at detecting, but he's the only man for the job when the FBI comes looking for someone to take on the Soviet-inspired DADA conspiracy.

Plus, he needs a paycheck. Chance gets off to a rough start as he's led on a merry chase through Chicago's underbelly and drawn into a case of deception that can only be solved with the help of a mysterious femme fatale who's as beautiful as she is cunning.

THE REGGIS ARMS CAPER

Try as he may, Chance Purdue can't seem to escape the world of private investigation. The now tavern owner returns to action to protect Princess Sonia of Kaleski, who claims to be the wife of an old Army buddy. Convinced he'll get to the bottom of things at his Army battalion's reunion, Chance indulges in the entertainment while leaving the more serious detective work to his new colleague, the scintillating Brandy Alexander. For Chance, the case provides more fun than intrigue, and yet its solution is a surprise for everyone involved.

THE STRANGER CITY CAPER

A quick and easy buck sounds good to Private Investigator Chance Purdue. But the paycheck seems to be a bit harder to earn when the job entails more than just looking into the a minor league baseball team in southern Illinois. His new client, the gangster Cool Lips Chericola, is definitely leaving out details. Enter Brandy Alexander, whose unexpected appearance in Stranger City, Illinois complicates things. Then throw in the Bobby Crackers'

Blitzkrieg for Christ religious crusade, and you've got a super-charged powderkeg of a caper, with Chance holding both the match and the barrel.

THE ABU WAHAB CAPER

What happens when Chicago detective Chance Purdue is hired to protect a gambler with a target on his head? For starters, all hell breaks loose...

"Bet-a-Bunch" Dugan is being hunted by International DADA (Destroy America, Destroy America) conspirators, a terrorist organization out for control of the world's oil market. Dugan needs more than a little luck to walk away unscathed. He needs a Chance, and though he knows that half of Purdue's reputation is that of a guy you are aching to punch, the other half is that he's a dogged, if occasionally doomed, investigator.

No matter where Purdue's leads take him, though, he always seems to be one step behind DADA. As a hapless Chance watches DADA's deadly scheme move forward, a siren named Brandy Alexander enters the picture and things finally fall into place, or so Chance hopes...

DEATH WORE GLOVES

When Sister Rosetta's niece goes missing, the nun (whose favorite poison is anything bottle-bound and boozy) hires shifty P.I. Tut Willow to find dear Gladys. But as Tut pulls back the curtain on Gladys' checkered past, he also finds that someone doesn't want her found, and soon bodies begin to pile up. Is Sister Rosetta, lured by a twisted sense of family loyalty, behind the deaths of those out to harm her niece, or are Tut and Gladys just pawns in a much darker game?

Full of laugh-out-loud comedy and the darkest of intrigue, the author of DEATH WORE GLOVES draws together femme fatales, a not-so-saintly nun, and a gumshoe willing to do anything to help an old flame.

KIRBY'S LAST CIRCUS

When the CIA chooses Birch Kirby, a mediocre detective with a personal life even less thrilling than his professional one, no one is more surprised by the selection than Birch himself. But the Agency needs someone for a secret mission, and Birch may be just the clown for the job. Going undercover as a circus performer, he travels to Grizzly Gulch to investigate the source of daily, un-decodeable secret messages that are being transmitted to the KGB. Birch interacts with wildly colorful characters while stumbling through performances as well as his assignment. With the clock ticking, Birch must hurry to take a right step toward bringing the curtain down on this very important case.

THE LACEY LOCKINGTON SERIES

THE FIFTH SCRIPT

Detective Lacey Lockington always gets the job done, but making the omelets of solved cases usually involves breaking a lot of eggs. So when Lacey gets suspended after tabloid columnist Stella Starbright names him as a "kill-crazy cop," he has to find new work as a private investigator. It's a step down, for sure, and one of his first cases is an unlikely one: former "Stella Starbrights" are turning up dead on the streets of Chicago, and the current one, the reputation ruiner herself, turns to an unlikely source for protection.

Going against his gut, Lacey agrees to keep tabs on Stella to keep her from sharing the grisly fate of her former namesakes. In the midst of all the madness, Lacey hunts the real killer, someone looking to silence gossip columnists for good. But can Lacey crack the case before another victim makes a different section of the newspapers?

Sex...violence...booze! This deadly mix will keep you on the edge of your seat in Ross Spencer's jaded-but-jaunty tale about a hardened cop with nothing but his reputation to lose.

THE DEVEREAX FILE

Former cop, now private investigator, Lacey Lockington gets lured into a case of something less smooth than his usual tipple: the death of his old drinking buddy and ex-CIA agent Rufe Devereaux. No sooner does he start his investigation than he finds himself chased by the Mafia, hunted by the CIA, stalked by a politician-turned-evangelist out to kill him and "helped" by the sultry Natasha, a KGB agent who always knows more than she lets on. Sucked into the dangerous world of international espionage, Lacey knows he is in way over his head. What started as a search for the truth behind his friend's death turns into a whirlwind tour that leads Lacey from the gritty bars of Chicago to Miami's cocaine-filled underbelly and culminates in an explosive ending that must be read to be believed!

THE FEDOROVICH FILE

The Cold War heats up when trouble comes knocking on the door of ex-cop turned Private Eye Lacey Lockington. Lacey is hot on the trail of Alexi Fedorovich after the high-ranking general publishes a controversial exposé detailing that Glasnost/Perestroika is a hoax. Federovich goes into hiding in the last place he suspects someone will look for him—somewhere in Youngstown, Ohio.

For someone who's pretty much seen and done it all, Lacey's unnerved when he starts dealing with Russian spies, Federal Agents, a man who doesn't want to be found, and an increasing body count of all his leads. Will Lacey, along with former KGB agent and live-in lover Natasha, get to the bottom of it all before Fedorovich finds himself on the wrong end of a firing squad?